YES!!
I HAVE A STORY

Compiled & Edited By
Rajeev Patel

INKQUILLS®

FOR THE READERS, BY THE WRITERS

Published by InkQuills Publishing House
www.inkquills.in

First Edition 2020

ISBN: 978-81-945636-1-7

ACKNOWLEDGEMENT

It's not just a book that you hold in your hand, it's someone's dream. This book has been possible due to the enormous love and support that people have given to us. It was their constant support that kept us going and ensured that we would be able to deliver it on time. We would like to thank each one of you from the bottom of the heart.

We would like to express our sincere appreciation and gratitude to:

i. Firstly, we would like to thanks our parents for belief in us. I know how tough it is to let your child fly high in the sky with the fear of what will happen if he falls.
ii. To all the friends who supported us in their journey.
iii. Big Thanks to my publisher "InkQuills Publishing House" and Abhisar Garg for believing in our work and delivering on time.
iv. All the Co-Authors who contributed their stories and believed us to go ahead.
v. The readers who are about to start the book. You all gave us the power to make our words reach to thousands of people out there.
vi. Lastly, God, who has constantly showered blessings on us.

ABOUT THE COMPILER CUM EDITOR

Rajeev Patel, 28, is a CA Dropout cum Digital Marketer.

He hails from the city of Raipur, Chhattisgarh but currently residing in city of dreams - Mumbai.

Writing was never his forte, it just came by chance. Though he is an avid Book Reader and Reviewer.

He hopes to inspire many more people. He is a Travel Enthusiast. Strong follower of 'KARMA'.

He can be reached out at –

Instagram- @itsrajeevpatel

Fb- Rajeev Patel & Mirakee - inkyour_thoughts,

Email Id - storytellerrajeev@gmail.com

CONTRIBUTING WRITERS

Brooke Walker H_2O!

(Adwika Tamrakar)

PROLOGUE

"Okay, you know what Ruthermace is planning.", A lady in a black dress said.

"Yes.", a man in a suit replied.

"If we don't stop him, all of Freyden will suffer."

"I am still not sure about my research. We need someone to go in and investigate."

"So, a spy?"

"No."

"Then?"

"Ruthermace's secret hideout is in the carnival. We can't just bust in and kill him, we don't want him to know we're after him."

"We have spies."

"Not a normal spy."

"What do you mean by that?"

"A kid spy."

BROOKE's A SPY

Autumn leaves fall, marking another nice day. People were cheerfully playing on their cycles and living life. They were playing a spy game.

Brooke was sitting in class, dwelling on what all she would do later.

She was having a nice day. At Hayfield Public School, life was going well for the 12 year-old. Well, not really.

She brushed her brown hair out of her eyes and tried to focus on learning the old tongue, Cor.

Shezuk mila hosek jimmain.

(Translation: I walked back home.)

Herosa ois moserst dase.

(Translation: She is eating food.)

"Yikes, how boring can Cor be?", She thought.

That's when the man entered.

"Brooke Walker, please stand up."

The uniform. Cops.

No. She wouldn't stand up. She couldn't. Her legs were like jelly.

"Brooke Walker, I repeat, please identify yourself."

She shakily stood up, her legs trembling. *Why do the police need me? Is it because I illegally used the blue dirt? I thought they wouldn't figure that out?*

“Brooke, we need you to come with us.”

She walked down the hallway of the police station until the police led her to a room.

“Sit here.”

She obliged.

“I'm Officer Barren.”

“N-Nice to meet you.”

“Nice to meet you too, Brooke. Now, do you know about your mom?”

“No?! What happened?”. A stunned silence.

“I'm sorry, but Brook Walker, your mother, Shannon Walker, previously Shannon Felicity, is dead.”

“What?! N-No. This isn't possible.”

“But it is.”

But the funny thing was, she didn't feel that much grief. Like, sure, her mom did take care of her and all that, but she didn't feel that much grief.

I guess it's because I know it's pointless to cry…

“So, now, as your only guardian is dead, you have two options.”

“Two?”

“The first one is to stay at the orphanage.”

“No Way.”

"And the second one?"

"Whatever it is, I don't wanna know. I choose the second one."

Mr. Barren seemed startled by her response.

"Are you sure, Brooke?"

"Yeah."

"Do you want to know what your option is?"

"Yeah."

"Your second option........ your second option is to be a spy."

Everything happened in a blur. Mr. Barren said that she had to sign a paper to be a spy. He said it was full of risks and near-death experiences. She didn't care. It all seemed cool in the Alex Rider books.

So she signed the paper.

"HEY, NO PRESSURE"

A few months later, after spy training.

"Okay, your first mission is to go to the carnival, bump into Ruthermace, act like a nice homeless kid, because if you do, he'll take you to his second house where he is nice enough to keep homeless kids. If you act really nice, he'll take you over to his literal house. There are currently only 2 kids in his first house, which is also the place where he resides." Said the lady, Mrs. Frost, Head of Department. Mr. Barren was also in the room.

"So I'm gonna go in unarmed?"

"No. Here are some things for you."

She gestured to a sorta sand covered necklace

"This is the only thing you ever had, from your fake mother, who died due to cancer. Push the amber bead once, a bomb will go off in 30 seconds."

She took out a piece of string and gestured to it.

"We know you're just a kid, but you're going in alone and we need to to have backup and self defence weapons, so this is a string. Tie a quick knot around a locked door, and it'll melt in seconds. Even the strongest locks."

She gestured to a piece of currency, Freyden's smallest one. The Vend.

"You have carry this. It's a tracking device, and if you're in trouble, just bite it, it will tell us and we'll come. It has been programmed to take only your saliva. It also contains a hidden camera and microphone, so we can see what is going on."

"Uh, can I just say that that's very weird?"

"No, you may not."

Well, it was worth a shot.

The lady walked out of the room.

“Hey, no pressure, ok?” Mr. Barren said.

“So I'm going on a mission, *alone*, to figure out what a criminal who's threatening the *whole* of Freyden is doing, risking my life, and I'm going without anything but a necklace, string and a *Vend?!?*”

“Uhhh… yeah?”

An awkward silence.

“Well, see you soon, kid. Remember, a lot of hopes are riding on ya.”, He said as he walked out.

THE MOST AWESOME FASHION SENSE IN FREYDEN

"Okay, it's time."

Brooke walked. No particular sense of direction, she just walked. She looked like a homeless beggar, many of which you find in Freyden's carnivals. but she was secretly scanning everyone that looked suspicious and everyone who didn't, too.

That's when she saw him. She had never seen him in person, but the photos had told her enough. Piercing green eyes, black Adidas and Dark blue sweatpants. Awesome fashion sense for a guy who wanted to destroy Freyden.

"Yup, that's him."

And he was heading right towards her.

She walked with her head low, acting like she didn't know where she was going. She neared his muscular body and then crashed into him, just like the plan said.

"O-Oh! I-I'm so sorry!!!" she yelped as soon as she jumped up. She picked up the basket and diamond necklace he was carrying and handed the basket to him.

"Are you okay?" he asked.

"Yes."

He stalked off. Brooke waited for a few seconds, keeping an eye on him, before running off in his direction, yelling, "Mister, mister!!"

"Yes?", He acknowledged.

"Mister, you forgot your necklace.", She said, handing it to him.

He looked startled.

"Well, thank you. Very few street children decide to give me back a precious diamond necklace! Since you are one of them, may I ask you a question?"

"Yeah."

"What happened to your parents?"

Silence.

"Mom's dead. Dad's been killed." She says quietly, faking sadness.

"I'm sorry for your loss. Since you have no parents, would you like to come and stay with me?"

She gasped, a fake gasp of happiness.

"Really?"

"Yes."

"Thank you! Thank you! Thank you!!!"

BIG HOUSES AND EAVESDROPPING

She walked with Ruthermace, who had introduced himself as Mr. John. He led her into a white marble house, and she swore she could see a ginormous swimming pool as she walked in. It was eerily quiet.

His assistant, who he had introduced as Mr. Benedict, seemed to be watching her every move.

As she lay on her bed, she held the Vend in front of her face.

She waved to it.

“I've got into the house and he's pretty dumb but his assistant's smart and there's a swimming pool and I'm pretty sure I can get out using the vents if I have to but this place's too big.” she said, hurriedly.

She walked out, deciding to spy on Ruthermace. She walked until she reached the door which Ruthermace had said was his.

“We gotta finish H_2O.”

“Now?”

“Yes.”

“Freyden, your time is running out. MWAHAHAHAHA!!!!!!”

She walked back into her room and closed the door. Just a few seconds later, there was a knock.

It was Ruthermace and his assistant.

“Listen, you gotta come to Dinner at 8:30 sharp, lunch at 1:20 sharp, and breakfast at 9:00 sharp, okay? And you're studying from 7:00 to 8:00, okay?” Ruthermace said.

“Yeah.”

Ruthermace was almost out of the door, when he stopped.

"Hey Harold- I- I mean Mr. Benedict, aren't you coming?"

"Let me just tell her the basic rules and regulations."

Ruthermace walked out, and almost immediately after, Mr. Benedict, or rather Harold, shut the door.

"Okay, girl. What's your name?"

"Ellie." She replied.

"Look, Mr. John is a top-secret villain, okay? He's keeping me as his slave, and I need your help to get out of here."

"What?! Why would he do that?! And why me?!" She yelped.

You could never be too careful as a spy.

"Because you look strong. And smart. And some of the other kids are robots. And the others are dead."

"LET'S JUST RANDOMLY LOCK BROOKE INTO A TORTURE MACHINE BACAUSE SHE EXISTS!!!"

A few days later, after Harold proved himself trustworthy of her secret by taking out one of the robot kids to figure out that they had tracking devices.

He led her to a dungeon, which she had no clue was there. "Okay, Ellie. I figured out that this dungeon can get us out.", He said, leading her into a bare room with nothing in it.

"Here?"

"Yup. Ruthemace told me it has a secret door, which can only be found by a child."

She walked around the room, inspecting every area. It had a lot of blood stains, and that was sort of creepy.

She heard a door slam shut behind her, capturing her in darkness.

"Mr.-Mr. B-Benedict?"

The room exploded in a burst of white light, blinding her.

Then a voice sounded, deep and robotic.

"Ellie, Daughter of Stella Mabel, is a traiter. YOU are a traitor, Brooke Walker. You are from unit Sp-Y of the mystery section of the government. That. Filthy. Government. It thinks it's sooooo smart, just putting the blue dirt out of civilian hands.

Yet when they use it for STUPIDNESS, they don't get killed. Yet when we use it for the greater good, they ARREST US AND KILL US?!!!!!!"

She shivered. There were only minutes till the crushing machine crushed her. It would be a gruesome death, with her toes crushed first, then her legs, then her torso.

M-My cover's blown?! What did I do?!

Machines came out of nowhere, blood illuminated on the sharp, needle point ends, as invisible ropes bound her and thrust her on a crushing machine which came out of nowhere.

W-Wait. The blood stains… This isn't a dungeon. This is a torture machine. And I've left all of the gadgets at my room!!!

Sharp machines that looked like they were gonna tear her heart out, (which they probably were), neared her.

Then she had a crazy idea.

One that would probably kill her.

Ehhhh,better than having herself crushed to death.

BROOKE ALMOST GETS KILLED

She wriggled up, standing on the conveyor belt.

Then she jumped onto the claw of the machine trying to kill her. It wriggled wildly, trying to kill her, but all she got was a scratch.

Then it wriggled even more, and she used its snapping mouth to cut off her binds.

Then she jumped free, jumping onto another snapping-killer-machine and using it to swing on top of the crusher.

Now, blood was leaking from her T-shirt, her lip, her nose, and she had bruises and scratches on her arms thanks to the snapping-killer-machines. She had seen something that looked similar to an off button, and she jumped up and slammed that.

The door swung open.

She coughed and spluttered. She hadn't expected it to be over this easily. Guess they were just dumb.

She walked down the hallway, looking each way for guards or someone that might've attacked her, but there was no one. She climbed up the stairs to her room, hoping to get back her stuff.

She walked in, and it was quiet. Eerily quiet. She grabbed her stuff and began to walk out.

Then the gunshots came, and someone injected her with something, and she felt herself losing consciousness.

"Mission H2O will take place in 30 minutes.", A voice said.

Brooke Walker woke up in an airplane seat.

"Don't let the girl escape."

A slurry of voices.

"Where are we?"

"Flying above Maraneds." answered Ruthermace.

Oh wait, I've been captured and there's this random thing called Mission H2O which is gonna happen in thirty minutes. I have all my stuff, but it's on that shelf over there, and I'm tied to the seat. And the necklace is all banged up. I can bite the Vend, but I gotta get it first.

I still have the string.

"LET'S JUST CUT UP PEOPLE'S CHEEKS BECAUSE THEY TALKED!"

"Sooooooooooo............ what's this Mission H2O?" She asked.

"A mission where we use the blue dirt's nitroglycerin to make a bomb that will destroy the whole of Freyden and it's stupidity."

Okay, that was very straightforward.

"Uhhhh..... Cool?"

"Speak again, and I'll kill you.", He said, holding up a knife.

Sometime later, she asked again, "Sooo, why d'you wanna destroy Freyden?"

She shouldn't have done that.

Harold walked up to her with a knife, and grabbed her face. Hard.

Then he very slowly dragged the knife across her cheek, making a bleeding gash.

She cried out in pain. Tears welled into her eyes as he did it the second time, and they poured out as he did it the third.

Now it was a bleeding cut.

"W-Where are we now?" She mumbled, not able to talk.

"Deltamause."

That's where the Sp-Y HQ is!! And I still have the string!!!! I can jump!!!!!!!!!!!

But what about the equipment?

She stood up.

"Where d'you think you're going?!" Ruthermace asked.

"Just, y'know, stretching my legs.", She replied, walking over to the door. They had untied her from the seat but her hands were still tied together.

"Don't try anything. It's the most securest lock ever."

"Even the strongest locks."

In the short amount of time where they looked away, she untied the rope from her arms. They were red and bruised, her cheek was bleeding and she had scratches all over.

She tied her string around the door.

"Hey!! What're you doing?!", Harold yelled.

But it was too late.

Brooke jumped out of a plane 15,000 meters high.

JUMPING OUT OF PLANE AT 15000 METERS IN THE AIR IS PERFECTLY NORMAL

She fell down, the sounds of gunshots whirling in the air behind her. The pressure was in her ears, so she closed them shut, like she had learnt in spy training.

I'm beginning to think this is a bad idea.

The Sp-Y unit wouldn't be able to see her, as the necklace was in the airplane.

And that's when the machines came.

They whirred in the air behind her. She turned around to see ginormous machines, which had a lot, and by a lot I mean a lot, of huge knives on them.

Uh-oh.

One charged at her, and she whirred off to the side to avoid it, kicking it in the process. It dropped down, destroyed.

Now people were beginning to point and stare.

Another one charged, and she whirred off to the side again.

But it had been expecting that. It took a sharp turn to the side, and she just barely had time to dive down.

It scratched her and she punched it. It flew off down, burning.

And she was near the ground.

If no one caught her, she would fall down, her body splattering against the pavement, her bones sticking out at awkward angles, a bloody mess all over.

Ugh, why do I have such a creative imagination.

That's when she lost consciousness.

EPILOGUE

Autumn leaves fall, marking another nice day. People were cheerfully playing on their cycles and living life. They were playing a spy game.

"He is destroying the world."

"You don't know how?"

"No."

"Do you know when?"

Brooke checked her watch, taking no interest in the many agents standing in front of her. Her eyes widened.

"Now."

You Are The Creator Of Your Own Destiny

(Anjali Jha)

The journey of life is not easy for all but to make it awesome and to fill with happiness and to make it like blossom of flowers, hard work, dedication and determination is required. To achieve success in our life and to make life comfortable we must have to believe on ourselves first. We must have to fill with positive thoughts and to walk on the road with enthusiasm, hope and faith on ourselves whether we are moving alone on the road and how hard the situation is but we must have to keep in mind that difficult roads always leads to beautiful destination. If nothing is permanent here, then nothing is also impossible here only we have to find our direction to change impossible into possible. Luck, faith and destiny all these can be changed by us if we work on it because the ray of hope always present inside the failure and if success is not final then failure is not fatal only we have that courage to continue our journey to count all these from failure to success.

Some things in our hand and we can do anything for it that we called it Karma and some things that are not in our hand that is in the hands of our Almighty and apart from this what we are doing and what will happen next after it is our destiny. But before doing if we think about our destiny and our future and we won't do that even what we can do is our faults and it's not our destiny's fault.

We have to fill ourselves with hope, courage and expectations. In short term our destiny can overcome us but in long term it won't work but we have to make our destiny. After every night there is day. After every ocean there is bank where we find land after the deepest ocean of water. After every tunnel there is an end where we can find light after passing from darkness. So, we have to rise ourselves with the light of expectations that "if sun sets in the west then the next day sun rises in the east."

If we look in this world then we see behind every successful person and behind their success stories there is painful and struggling stories of past. Some people walk on the open road just along with hope and expectations. Sometimes they are so lonely that they are even ditched by their family and society but they never look back because they have confidence on themselves that they will do it what they want to do in life. They know it very well that they are the creator of their own destiny.

Varun was born in a poor class family and he was first child of her parents among their four children. His mother was house wife and his father was running his own bicycle repairing shop outside his village. Life was not so smooth as in his family there was only one earner and there were six members in his family. So, it's difficult to provide food, shelter, clothes, medicine, education and everything from his father's hard earned money. They were living in a single room. Life was very complicated but they were happy in what God has given to them. All children were enjoying their life with their own style.

Varun was very intelligent from his childhood. He had special interest in science and study. He was growing day by day among his four sisters. When he grew then he also helped his father at his shop after his school and study. They were living in scarcity of everything but they didn't utter a word to their parents. They got only one clothes in the whole on the occasion of Holi but they didn't ask their parents for more in a year but they were happy with it.

Now he also started his study and started going to school but due to money he went to government school. He was not able to pay for books and copies. Sometimes he became very curious to see his textbooks but he couldn't purchase. One day he decided to go to his friend's house to read with him. Aniket was his best friend in his village. So, he invited him to come to his home. After reaching at home, he was very excited to go to his home. He instantly ate some food and ran towards his home and Aniket was also waiting for him to study together.

Both went inside home and started studying. At that time his mother went to market with her friends for shopping, so he was alone at home. After an hour his mother came and she saw Varun was sitting on Aniket's bed and both were engrossed in study. When she saw this scene, she became angry on her child. She suddenly rushed towards his room and slapped him hardly. Slapping was so hard that her hand left five fingers print on his cheek. Both stunned for a while and couldn't utter a word. Both were nervous that why she slapped him so hard without asking and giving any warning. Again she continued, "Do you know?" Who is he? Aniket said, "Yes I know, he is Varun and he is my best friend. He had no books and he can't buy, so I asked him to come here." Again, she said, Huh……… He is your best friend and not mine. I don't like to allow to come and to sit in my room to a stranger. And one more thing he is stranger for me as well as what's his status? Uska aukad hi kya hai mere samne, baap iska cycle punchar banata hai aur beta chala hai IAS bnne. Aree IAS bhi to IAS ka hi beta banta hai bhikhari ka nhi. Padh ke hi kya kr lega…. Jyada se jyada baap se bara dukan khol lega aur kuhh nhi. (What's his status infront of me? His father makes bicycle puncture and the the son has gone to become an IAS officer. Hey, IAS officer also becomes the son of an IAS, not a beggar's son. What he will do after studying. He will do more than he will open a shop bigger than his father). After listening all these he couldn't speak a word but tears were rolling down from his eyes. He was not in a condition to either sit there or to leave them at that moment.

But for him, Aniket started quarrelling with his mother. Again his mother started beating him and also warned him that she will complaint for this to his father. But he had no effect of this, he was continuously weeping and cursing to his mother for doing like this. After all this Varun came forward to wipe his tears and gave sympathy and finally left his home. In between this when he was walking on road and moving towards his home, only one thought was running in his mind. Neither he was cursing his destiny nor he was cursing to his parents about their status due to which he was insulted by her.

Necessity is the mother of invention. In this universe, everything was originated by living beings only when they had lack of something. Without need we can't do anything because our mind couldn't focus on that need if we have everything in our life. Sometimes we do a work and its completed successfully and we gave credit for this to ourselves but in reality we do only our half part and other part is completed by this whole universe in different forms. Everything happens in this world is only due to reason. If we have no question, then we have no any answer. So, just to give answer first we have to search question and only then we can proceed. Nothing is permanent and nothing is impossible. Only we have to analyses ourselves in every situation and we have to work towards our lack because never a misery undeserved and there never has been an evil, for which we didn't pave the way with our own hands. But after all these analyses we come to a point where I find a ray of hope and that ray says us that we have no control of the external world, but that which is in me and nearest on to me and my own world is in my control and that's my destiny.

Just thinking all these during his journey from Aniket's home to his own home finally he decided to do something best in his life. Yes, his journey started from there. He made himself strong for this and isolated himself from the world just to bring positivity inside himself. He knew that he couldn't achieve what he wants in his life alone because success is what it's a combination of both success and failure and for this he has to learn from people and negativity to make himself more strong. Just he has to keep patience for himself, just he has to work persistently, he has to work with perspiration to make an unbeatable combination for success.

After all what happened to him, he didn't say to anyone in his family. But he changed now. He started working hard. He was continuous in his work. But sometimes when we want to move forward then our fate is also against of this but we have to work against our fate just to achieve our real success because we are the creator of our destiny and we have to work in such a way that even one time what our fate was against us will be in our favour.

He was in class 9th when his father became seriously ill. He was admitted in a hospital for few days but due to lack of money he was discharged from that hospital. In between this a doctor from government hospital helped him a lot. He came for regular checkups. Now his mother started working on shop and he also helped his mother in this. At home his sisters were taking care of his father. In this situation it was very difficult for him to continue his study but to pursue his dreams, he continued. Her sisters were also educated upto matriculation, so they helped him in his study. He continued his study and just gulping down all his problems he finally sat in matriculation examination. His exam lasted in February on 23rd and now he was free from his first stage hurdle.

It was 27th February when his father finally left this world after his prolonged illness. He was suffering from cancer and due to lack of treatment they couldn't save him. Now everything ended in his life without completion. All burden came on his head. He gave up his dreams and decided to leave his study and to continue his father's work.

He started working on the shop along with his mother. After two months his result was out and he topped in his school. Now a ray of hope came in front of him. His mother and sister supported him to continue his study. But next problem arised now to take admission in which college. He got a college in which he had to pay ten thousand in advance for two years course. But he couldn't give such large amount so again he decided to leave his dreams. One day he sat on his shop and his mother was also sitting there. Suddenly the doctor came who was treating his father and he was also going for admission of his children. He asked him, “Whatsup?” He said, Nothing so much, as usual sir. Life is just going on track. He asked about his study and then he explained everything. Then the doctor instantly gave him ten thousand from his pocket and advised him to take admission.

He instantly rushed towards the college. Till that time second list was also ready to announce the student’s admission list. He prayed to take his admission. Finally, he took admission there and started his journey. Two years’ life was the toughest phase of his life. He woke up early in the morning at 6 O’clock. At 7 O’clock his classes started and he returned to home at 1 pm. After that he went to teach students in a tuition and it continued for 10 pm in the night. After that he came to his shop for ledger purpose and after completing work there he reached to home and after that he started studying for two to three am in the morning and only after that he was sleeping. His sisters were also teaching in a village and everyone was working hard. In this way their life was running. Finally, he completed his intermediate and also gave CEE examination in which he got 180 marks out of 200. And he got selected in NIT for engineering.

But to shape his career in engineering was not easy for him. He was not able to pay fee in engineering college. Apart from college fee he had to pay seventy thousand for hostel and mess. He decided not to pay money for that whether what will be the outcomes. Anyway he took admission there and fee was paid by his mother which she earned in two years. His sisters earned in tuitions and also he earned in his salary and also through his friends. He adjusted his first year fee of total one lakh budget. Finally, he left his home and shifted in college hostel.

Again same thing he decided that anyway he has submitted first year but now he won’t for the next year fee. He came there with positivity but when he came their and talked to some seniors and batch mates they said what to him, "Do you know?" Without backlogs you can't complete your engineering. If you complete this without backlog, then people will think that you have not studied engineering. Some toppers are also present but they are of another world. After listening all these rumors, he became sad and also he was afraid after thinking for his conditions. Anyway he started his study there even after listening all rumors. He decided to study in his fulltime and not to put himself in any extra-curricular activities. Six months passed, so his first semester exam completed. Finally, he got eighty-six percentage marks that was obviously highest at that time. Maybe that record was broken by someone now but at that it has some other value.

After his result he came into existence in his college as everyone of his college from student to teacher and all staffs came to know about him. Now everyone started counting him in genius.

But again next problem started and that problem was of fee. He again decided that not to pay fee in this time anyway. Because he had no option to fee in this time. Till now his pocket money was paid by his friends. Then he decided to talk to his principal, Dean and admission department of his college, so that he can get some way to waived his college fee.

One day he met to Mrs. Sukanya Sinha who was assistant professor of mathematics department in his college. She was his teacher as well she was his Rakhi sister as she tied him Rakhi so he also gave credit of sister. He told her all his problems of his family. She decided to help him in his study. First she informed about him to principal, dean, vice Chancellor and all departments of his college about him. And this matter spread like fire of jungle. She asked them to give Mercy for his fee as he was not able in the next session but to process all these it took one year and finally he entered in next semester. Till now his friends and his professor Mrs. Sukanya Sinha paid his fee and all.

In this he completed his four years of college. In the next and final year of his college, companies started coming for campus placements. Before placements final result from University has also arrived and he was University topper. He was University Gold medalist.

Apart from this during placements he got opportunities from six companies. He was the one in his college who completed his engineering degree without any backlogs and got opportunities from six companies at a time.

During this he met a professor of IIT Delhi who asked him for his future plans and asked him to give exam of GATE. He accepted this and prepared himself for this in only four months. He sat in examination and secured his seat in GATE examination and also got a seat in IIT Bombay.

Again after this his college organized two days' seminar in which a met Dr. Surendra Iyyar who was scientist at DRDO. He asked him for IES (Indian Engineering Services) examination. He was ready for this too. Now he had only five months for his IES examination. He took syllabus and book for preparation. He started his preparation. When he took syllabus of that examination he was sure that he will crack this examination because he saw the whole syllabus was same as the syllabus of his four-year engineering degree program. In this way he prepared for four months for IES examination. Now examination was about to commence in next month but again his plan changed when he met an IAS officer in his district. He was truly motivated by him. He came to know about IAS that it's the most prestigious examination and job in our country.

Again he left his IES preparation and decided first and last to be an IAS officer but now his mother changed her decision and she became angry on him. He has not talked to him for few months. As she asked him to join his job rather than studying more now because his family's condition became worst now.

His mother convincing him to join his job but he left all his options when he decided to join his job till that time date has passed. But at last his mother was ready to help him in IAS preparation. He started his preparation. When he started his preparation till that time he had only four months left for prelims examination. Anyway he started his preparation just keeping himself engrossed only in books and syllabus.

Four months passed and his exam date has arrived. He was prepared himself very well to sit in the examination. Finally, he sat in examination and completed his prelims examination. After prelims he had only six months' time for his mains examination. Now he has to select his optional for the preparation of mains examination. But now he was sometimes sinking in the subjects selection and sometimes he was diving in the course syllabus. He was unable to select his subjects. First he took geography. When he read only first four pages everything became out of his mind. Then he took other subjects one by one. Sometimes he was taking philosophy, sometimes he was taking history, sometimes economics. Till that time his prelims result was out and he has qualified his prelims examination. Now he has to select his best optional subject and he has to work hard. Then he went to meet his mentor and asked for subject selection. He advised him to choose political science. He took and tried to understand the subject but now his wait came to an end. Finally, he chose political science as optional subject and started his preparation. He was hard worker as well as he did smart study for the preparation of examination. Every day he was about to cover some topics and for this he made a study plan and he completed every backlogs in the next even he has to cover more topics on the next day but he never took his leg behind from his preparation and hard work. It was his dedication. It was his passion.

After six months of hard work it was the day of mains examination. In the first sitting it was his GS paper but unfortunately he couldn't do well in the examination. He came outside the examination hall in frustrated condition. He was so sad that he was continuously weeping in the leisure time between first sitting and second sitting examination.

In between this, he sat in next sitting in which optional subject examination has to be held. Do you know if you are honest with yourself as well as with your work then no one can change your destiny. If you are going to make your own path, your own destiny then it maybe you have to pass a lot of hurdles but no one can change your path. Yes, he was very honest in his work from his childhood. He loved to study from his own notes and for this he always made his own notes. He was very talented in making notes and distributing it to his friends. He has also mentored several friends in making notes and today all his deeds of past helped him a lot.

He was sure that he won't select in first attempt. So he was sad for this and he was cursing himself for his destiny's job. But miracles always happens suddenly. You can't estimate your destiny's deeds. But it always works on its time. Yes, when he got news of mains result first he couldn't believe on his ears but when he asked again and his friend repeated again then he was on cloud nine. He secured 32 rank in mains exam and he was hearing what was 3200. He was in difference of two digits. He was still not believing on himself because he was remembering that he has not attempted more questions in GS paper but how this miracle happened?

Then his mentor said to him that here how many questions you have attempted didn't matter but here only how well you have answered all those questions mattered in ranking of students. His way of writing each and every answer helped him in getting this position. After seven years a ray of hope and the beam of happiness was blinking in his home. His mother and sisters were proud on himself. He was the one who is going to change his destiny through his deeds.

Finally, after mains examination it was the time for interview. Till now everything he got in his life what he wants in his life. But for interview he was very nervous for his interview. But it went very well and finally his dream came true. A poor boy from a poor family without his father today got success in India's prestigious examination which is the dream of several youths. A boy who was thrown out from his friend's home by his mother but today she is that lady who came in his office to take help from him. It's not a miracle that his destiny changed but all these became possible for him only due to his hard work, dedication and determination took him here. He is the creator of his own destiny.

Everything is possible in this world only if we work ourselves in this direction to achieve our dreams. We work for our journey to achieve destination. We shape our future through our work and no one can do it for us. We create our own destiny by the way we do things. We have to take these opportunities and be responsible for our choices because a slight mistake can change our life for forever.

"We write our own destiny. We become only what we do. We are the decider of our own destiny and the inventor of our identity. We create our own story and perhaps more importantly we also write our last chapter of our story."

Nightmare
(Ankita Saloni)

Her mind was constantly replaying that memory, just like a music player playing an audio, on a repeat mode. She wanted to escape, but she couldn't. She wanted to hide, but she couldn't. All she had were those terrible memories of her hiding when one day suddenly, the world turned against them.

It was a fine evening and she was enjoying snacks on her couch when a news reporter announced the initiation of World War by two rival countries. Soon after that, their life changed. The business of her father slowed down and on the verge of bankruptcy, he was forced to sell everything that he once possessed. He was unable to pay the loan that was sanctioned to him and in such a sensitive situation, when there was a large outcry amongst the common people for food and money, the Bank was forced to file a complaint against him. It gave police the power to arrest him as soon as possible until and unless he repays the loan.

To keep his family alive in such a dangerous situation was the biggest challenge for her father. But somehow, he managed to find a place of their hiding with the assistance of some of his acquaintances.

Their life became a living hell and they were forced to keep themselves safe and alive by any possible means.

But it all came for a price. A price that was too hard for them to pay.

Her grandfather died soon after because they were not in a condition to afford his treatment due to the sudden rise in cost of surgeries.

With moist eyes, they bid him goodbye, with a regret in their heart. A regret that they could've saved him but they didn't.

But this was just the beginning for them. The worst days were yet to come.

Things started deteriorating day by day. There was an acute shortage of food and they witnessed many nights, when they had no other options than to sleep hungry. Earlier, she was so fond of sun. But now, all her days were engulfed in darkness. A darkness that never seemed to end and day by day, it was creeping into every corner of their hiding. She always felt being watched, like someone was lurking in the shadows, beneath the bed, inside the creaking closet, behind the curtains, and almost everywhere in that place. Her mind started playing tricks with her.

She prayed to the God to mend everything that went so terribly wrong. She used to miss those beautiful evenings when she used to play with her friends in the city park. And the annual days in her school where she won numerous accolades in Dancing competition. And the beautiful gown that she wore on her last birthday for which she got the compliment of being a "Beautiful princess" from one of her favourite aunts.

Now all she had were dull and old clothes that they managed to gather from the leftovers after their house was burnt during the airplane bombing. They became homeless and their life escalated from riches to rags really fast.

In a shabby and stinky place, they somehow managed to remain alive.

It all felt terrible to her. A person like her, who used to have luxurious cushions at her home once, was now sleeping on the floor. One whose tongue was accustomed to taste only the best of delicacies, was forced to eat the leftover food in order to remain alive. Only if she could tell someone, how much does she hate her current situation. She desperately wanted to die, but couldn't. She wanted to break free of all the shackles, but unfortunately, she couldn't.

She couldn't sleep at night. The floor appeared so harsh and cold to her. How can she even sleep on such a thing? One night, she decided to escape from that hell, either by hook or by crook. But the very next moment, she looked at her mother, who was lying beside her. Even after being heavily pregnant, she wasn't getting proper medicines and check-ups as they weren't able to afford anything else besides some milk and vegetables.

Tears resurfaced in her eyes and she cursed everyone for their current situation.

"What a pathetic government!!!", anger was visible in her eyes but she knew, that she can't mend the things. All she can do is to suffer… with her family.

She used to read a book occasionally that her father gifted her on her birthday once and that book was "The Diary of a young girl". Never had she thought, that she is going to relive all those moments that Anne Frank and her family did. She could relate how painful it is for someone to helplessly watch their whole world crumbling in front of their eyes, their loved ones being snatched away from them, and knowing that they can't do anything to save them. All that they can do is silently shed tears as the pain goes on and on.

One fine day, she was helping her mother in preparing meal when all of a sudden, her mother moaned out of pain.

"Call your father. This pain is unbearable.", she managed to blurt out while holding her hand. She rushed to find him but then she remembered, she couldn't even shout his name. They were in hiding and even a small act of negligence could lead them to the Jail, a place where thousands of innocent civilians were being killed every day for no reason. With tears of fear being strolling down her cheeks, she tried to make her way with the help of a candle and while she finally managed to reach the main door, she heard a loud moan and *thud*. Everything was quiet after that.

Her mind sensed what was wrong. Candle fell out of her hand and she rushed towards her mother. Her mother was lying in a pool of blood and finally after so long, she was in peace.

She couldn't bear to lose her mother like that as she meant the whole world to her. She cried, she pleaded, she begged, but her mother didn't listen. This trait of hers made her the worst mother in the history of motherhood. The girl made all the promises that she could remember but to no avail. Her mother turned deaf to all her pleas.

Now, her father was her only hope. The sole reason for her to stay alive in this cruel world. But she still didn't know how to break this news to him.

Just then, she heard a knock on the door. She panicked but somehow managed to open it.

Her uncle was standing in front of her. His expressions dropped a hint that something was terribly wrong. But what? She had no idea about.

“Oh Dear! I don't know how to break this news to you. But your father. While he went to visit one of his friends to arrange some money for your mother's medicine, a police officer saw him and ordered to arrest him at that instant. He ran and managed to escape but the next moment, he got hit by a speeding car and died at that spot. Please don't tell this to your mother. She won't be able to bear this in that condition. You are getting what I'm saying right. Ohh my poor child. May God rest him in peace.”

She wasn't listening anymore. Her mind wasn't able to figure out anything. Everything started blacking out. Her world has shattered in a moment. Every thought in her mind faded and all she remembered was the worried face of her uncle, before falling unconsciously on the floor.

She woke up, covered in cold sweat. She was panting uncontrollably. She was unable to believe that whatever just happened was real or not.

After a few minutes, she came back to her senses and noticed everything is normal, as usual that it should be.

"Ohh my god, such a terrible nightmare...", she took a sigh of relief.

She then went towards the kitchen to fetch a glass of water and after grabbing a bowl of fruits, she turned on the TV and sat on the couch.

As she was reshuffling the channels, she came across a News channel that was flashing her favourite advertisement.

Soon the advertisement was cut short, and a figure appeared on the screen with breaking news in background.

"This is an emergency update."

The bowl of fruits fell from hands as soon as she heard those words, "The government has announced an emergency and there are very high chances that a World War can happen anytime soon."

Missing Dad
(Anshika Kodukula)

Vaishnavi was a small girl who was born and living in Nochikuppam, Chennai. Though she was poor, she was prosperously rich in academics. She was a dad's doll and often towards dad's side. After the school hours, she used to spend most of her time talking with her dad about what happened in school, how was she doing her work and the rest of the time with her cute little buddies making castles and playing with marbles in the Marina beach. She was so brilliant that she was very curious to know about how her father caught hold of fish and the different types of fish which are differentiated on the basis of the scales present on them. Yadmma was an innocent lady who would go for 5-6 houses for working.

"Appa, won't you go for fishing today?" questioned Vaishnavi, she also added, "It's likely to rain outside." "Though the weather is ominous, I need to go Vaishu. I will return back right. I will bring a biiiiiiiggggg fiiisssshh for you, mom will cook it deliciously and we all will have it! Don't worry. In the meanwhile you be ready completing your homework. I will be at home soon." said Sreenivas, the fisherman.

He waved to his wife, Yadamma and went to the shore of Marina beach and set sail. No sooner had he set the sail, then it started raining. The glowing spume on the crystal blue water vanished and the tides came up with huge amount of force where the boat was likely to drown. Sreenu thought that this was not the right time for him to go fishing and started returning back to the shore. It was the time when he got reminded of the words which he told to Vaishnavi that he's gonna bring a fish which will be the supper but he, in that typical situation, seemed helpless.

"Appa, a fish for me?" asked the poor girl out of super excitement when she saw a cover held by Sreenu. "I'm sorry dear!! It's raining outside. One fish to you is due for tomorrow Vaishu. Let's eat this yummy coconut chutney today. I'll bring that to you tomorrow. Okay.?" said Sreenu despondently out of pain. Sreenu was very sad that he couldn't fulfil his daughter's wish of bringing her favourite. The girl nodded her head disappointedly and they three started their meal.

After that, before sleeping, Yadamma exclaimed, "Sreenu, I'm not getting enough money for the heavy work I do. Let us go back to our place, Yelamanchili, and do some labour work there itself. We will get money and we can also live happily." Sreenu slept of exhaustion by the time Yadamma was about to complete her words. That was their routine and they were in a complete state of poverty where they don't even have money to run their livelihood.

They get their one-time meal only if they work hard and earn the money. They spent a number of days without having food but in those bitter circumstances too, they kept their daughter, Vaishnavi, happy. They filled her stomach and remained fasting for many many end-less nights. Sreenu often thought only of getting the fish with which he could keep his family happy and fulfil their necessities to the fullest extent.

"Bye appa!! Bring a fish today at least...." asked Vaishnavi to her dad. He answered boldly, "I'll surely bring it for you today Vaishu.... I promise you, today's supper for us is fish curry."

She left to school with a charming smile on her face. Vaishnavi went to school and there too, she was merrily telling to her friends that her dad is gonna bring fish and she will eat it. She was also telling her friends proudly that her dad does everything that she wants. As the sun started brightening its beam, Sreenu started fishing. Due to the intensity of the sun, Sreenu's eyes showed him a blur fish moving up and down. Though he was having a sensation of dizziness, Sreenu was highly determined to catch a fish and take it to Vaishu. Unfortunately, he fainted.

Vaishu returned abode and without changing her clothes, sat in the verandah waiting for her dad. "Vaishu, go change your clothes... Freshup..." when Yadamma said, "Amma, appa will return home now. He told me that he'll bring me a fish. He still hasn't arrived. I'll fresh up after appa comes." Vaishu answered. Sreenu, by taking the help of his friend, came home without anything in his hands. Vaishu questioned "Appa, my fish???" Sreenu replied, "Vaishu, I haven't found any fish today. That's why I brought this for you." He took out a thin chain from his pocket and gave her. "Thank you appa!" hugs her dad in gratitude. Infact, that was Sreenu's chain., he gave it to her.

"Come Vaishu, have lunch. I've kept rasam rice there. Eat it fast., you need to sleep now." commanded Yadamma when Vaishu nodded her head saying NO. "Vaishu, if you eat this, you'll get so much energy. We both will play in the beach together later. Come on, have this." Sreenu fed to Vaishu. She ate happily and slept. Yadamma told, "Sreenu, you know what, though Vaishu spends less time with you, she has abundant love and affection towards you. She always thinks about you. Whenever i ask anything, after telling what it is, she relates that incident with you in some or the other way for sure. She admires you profusely."

Days passed on, there was progress in the field of technology but not in the lives of Sreenu, Yadamma and Vaishnavi. And, due to various circumstances, the promise of fish for Vaishu is not yet fulfilled.

Like every day, Sreenu went on sailing and promised her that he will return back. The sun slowly set but there were no fish found. As it was the month of September, it was obvious that it will rain and the same happened. The weather turned on storm. Flashing lights on the sky created a panic situation. This was treacherous and a feeling of fear developed in Sreenu. He was totally clear that he is gonna breathe for the last time at that moment. His whole life was once rewinded and visible in front of his eyes. That's it and he's all gone!

Vaishnavi and Yadamma were looking forward for Sreenu to arrive, especially his daughter for her fish to come soon. Yadamma was in despair. As the days flew, Vaishu stopped going to school and started to sit beside her mother selling precious stones in the beach. She would look at that wrinkled water with hope that her dad, Sreenu would come back some day with a fish for her. Vaishu still remembers that Sreenu would tell that the sky is not the only limit and try to look beyond the horizon even. She was never in despair that her dad is not going to return at all but every day, she still has a hope and searches for her 'missing dad', holding her chain tightly which was his only memory for her, as the sun spreads its yellowish-orange glow to its blue brother saying goodbye to the dark.

The Woman With Twelve fingers And A Wart

(Avijit Roy)

"Believe me, she is a witch", Caroline said, supported emphatically by Bob's nodding.

"She must have twelve fingers and an eye on her forehead", Draco said trembling.

The other children agreed because there was hardly any strong point to dispute.

What the children took to be a closed eye on the woman's forehead was really a big black wart. She looked unusual, even frightening to the village children, and her dark stained teeth that would often peek out while she parted her dry lips, added to her horrific appearance.

Three years ago, it was winter and the children were counting days for Christmas celebration when the lady appeared in the village from nowhere. Age had grown on her skin like moss on a stone. Children started to weave tales about her mysterious arrival.

She accommodated herself in a dilapidated and deserted house enveloped by shrubs and trees at the fringe of the village. A few of the villagers, being curious, had asked her, "Who are you?"

She had smirked in an ugly manner that sat on the listeners' nerves.

"Why are you here in this haunted house?" one from the group inquired.

Her face turned grave as if clouds had gathered, and she mildly shook her head before muttering, "This is my last birth place."

Her words felt unsettling upon their wit. One of them wondered, "Last birth place! What do you mean?"

"I have been living for many, many ages, taking different forms in different places. Years ago I was born here."

Such eerie words didn't repel the listeners, rather instilled a belief in them that she was an insane. She was left in her crumpled world for she was deemed a harmless intruder.

"Look, the witch comes", children would cry seeing her coming down the lanes, and rolling her eyes and twisting her fingers like spider's legs, she would frighten them away. She frantically tried to call them back, but her unrestrained gesture would shoo them further away. Caroline was most affected.

She never begged from anyone, and the people who had termed it as "impoverished dignity" would sympathize, and they didn't let her starve as they felt the urge of humanity in them.

"Why do you all feed that witch?", Caroline demanded of her mother who had been packing a parcel of bred and boiled egg for the stranger woman.

"Why not, darling? And don't call her a witch. She is a woman with some deformities. More of that she is of your granny's age."

"No, she is a witch, and one day she will devour us all. Have you ever seen one with three eyes?" The little girl warned, which evoked laughter from her mother.

Then it really happened one day when the daylight had yielded to darkness, Caroline didn't return from school. Words went around the village, and Caroline's mother held the witch-woman responsible. She was inclined to the speculation because this strange woman was the easiest suspect, even if the accusation was not rational. Some other who had their conjecture aligned with Caroline's mother decided to invade her shelter.

"The girl was always frightened of that weird woman. She might have...", Caroline's mother's voice choked as she visualized some terrifying images.

When the village folk led by Caroline's mother reached the woman's house, it was enveloped by impregnable darkness. Only faint candle light was flickering out of a broken window, making it seem like the pounding heart of a dark beast.

"Are you in, lady?" one of the villagers shouted at the silent interior.

A shadow was detected moving inside and as it limped outward, everyone held their breath.

"Where's Caroline, my daughter?" Caroline's mother implored in tears.

The woman in tattered clothes stood silent, as if endeavoring to arrange her jumbling words.

"Caroline", someone from the confronting crowd repeated loudly.

The old woman was shaken, having been startled during her meditation. She smirked in an ugly way.

"Give my child back", Caroline's mother commanded.

"You!!! ugly bitch, give the child back", someone screamed to join the urge.

"I know, I know", the old woman giggled.

Everyone's heart skipped a beat as the impatience manifested in every pair of eyes.

In the following silence the woman said, her voice shaking, "I was born here ages ago. I know all the secrets. I know the old truths."

"Return the child, or...", a man from the crowd threatened while others got ready to pounce on her. The wretched woman shrunk back. Their belief had somehow staggered. No one thought of her as insane—they wanted to think the worse.

Suddenly a voice intruded from the darkened woods from behind the crowd.

"Mom, I'm here."

It was Caroline, safe but all covered in dirt.

"Where were you?" her mother rushed to her, heaving breaths of relief.

"I decided to make a surprise visit to Mia's house. It was her birthday, Mom. I'm sorry. It was so sudden, I hurried and in dark I slipped..."

Her mother wrapped Caroline in her warm and welcoming arms before she could finish her explanation as her tears loosened all restraint.

"I know the secrets. I know the truths..." uttering the words like a hymn the old lady moved inside the womb of the engulfing darkness. The village folk looked at each other, sharing their embarrassment of judging this woman—and being so wrong. The darkness around seemed to thicken on their hearts.

The Academics
(Feroz Shaik)

I didn't have amazingly good grades. So, I was sent away from home. It was my second year at a boarding school by then I was fifteen. Room no. 8 was mine. Outside the window, the coral tree had occupied much space. The branches of the tree were thick with scarlet, pea-shaped flowers. Crows, mynahs and parrots would be seen perched on this tree, these soon became my friends. I had spent many evenings watching them. Football, shorts and dark chocolates had always been with me. I never had interest to by hard those lengthy answers, consequently my results weren't up to the mark.

Saturday at four o'clock in the evening, there was a knock at the door. When I opened the door, I was stunned to see "Ram."

Ram, the assistant to the Principal. He had almost the same tone of a commanding officer, which doesn't suit his personality. He was dark and short in height. He was the one who had issued notices to many students on various grounds. "Raghav, your notice," said Ram. I was shocked and shivered with fear. "Raghav, your notice", he said as he reached out his arm, the paper somehow slipped away from my hands. Quickly I slammed the door when Ram left my place. I sat on the floor and began to read the notice. My body became hot after reading it.

The night had been horribly hot and I slept on the floor. I woke up by the hardest kiss of a mosquito. Light and fan stopped working due to power cut. Mosquitoes had a grand feast sucking my blood. This dark moment took me into the darkest world. There was so much on my mind which was racing a hundred miles per hour. All I had was the fear to face mom with my low grades. I can't live up to my mom's expectations.

Early in the morning, all the boys were out with their luggage to spend the vacation. By 7am all left the school. I was watching at the clock in the hall and spent the time by feeding broken biscuits to the Principal's dog. At 8am my father came to pick me up. I wasn't comfortable in the car; dad asked me, “How did you write exams?” “Yes dad, of course well”, I answered him. The two hours’ journey was so awkward filled with fear.

“Hey mom, how are you doing?” I said. Mom kissed my forehead and hugged me. “I’m fine my baby” replied mom. I was wondering why mom didn't ask me about my marks. Later I had learnt that she was busy with too many works with regards to my uncle's marriage. There was still two solid hours of time to attend the marriage. So I took out my love, football. It was then the ball flew on air and landed on the table. Huge breaking sound dragged my mom. She had knocked at the door. In no time I opened the door. “What was the sound?” She asked. I pretended and said, “Sound? No, nothing mom.” She pushed off back. After an hour she began to search for her watch. I tried to be innocent and was away from the scene.

She was upset and tears were rolling down. I asked “is it because of the missing watch?” She nodded her head. I went back to my room, pulled out the watch from my bag. Later, arranged those two pieces together and placed on the table. I held my mom’s hand, brought to my room to show the watch on the table. It was her favourite watch gifted by her father. When she gently took into her hand, the other piece was remained at the same place. That's all....... She ran behind me to catch. She couldn't chase me and I gave up. She pulled my ears and said, “You deserve a punishment, get A grades in all the subjects.” Ahhhh was my sound. After all every mother wants good grades at the end.

After few days, I dared to give the letter to my parents which was written by the Principal, Mehra. He was very serious and never gave me a chance to speak to him. I wanted to tell him that I don't want to mug up and create miracles. I had no dare to enter to his room. I was crazy and couldn't figure it out how to and what to do. My mom said, "You better wash dishes at home and stop everything." She didn't mean it but…

Gradually I became a slow learner at the boarding school. One day, I was astonished to see my parents in the school. I did go near them but they didn't allow me. Ram, called them in. I was anxious about what could be the reason for their arrival at the school.

Ram got my luggage from the room. My parents pushed me in car and drove off.

After six months, I was taken to a new school. My parents made me determine and work hard in these six months and of course there was improvement and I impressed them and won their hearts in no time. I was doing well in all the aspects.

After a year when I joined the school, things began to take another direction. I didn't know what exactly I turned up to. My heart dropped when my dad said, "Where's your report card?" I sucked my teeth. I took time to get back. Before I handed it to my dad I said, "Sorry" averting my eyes. He gave a scowl look and said, "You need to fix this." It was actually my mistake; I hadn't done my best. I couldn't figure it out how my grades had gradually fallen down. I screwed up everything, just zipped my mouth and shed tears. I determined to keep full stop and move ahead. Overnight I mustered up the courage for the plan of action. "Hey my little heart, won't you ask me what's going on?" Anusha, was one of the most beautiful girls in my school. Her big eyes and wonderful smile made her the prettiest girl in my section. She also, was the only girl with good traditional values. Every time I looked at her I felt like telling her about my feelings for her. Man!!! She was the most awesome girl in the whole of standard 9th, St. Andrews Public School. My mind was filled with several questions of how to impress her and tell that how much I liked her. I sorted several ways to express my love but nothing seemed right. At last I decided to tell her directly during the lunch break. I skipped an hour and had my lunch to get free time during lunch. Lunch was the only time we exchanged secrets. So, some of my mates were busy in gossiping while others were playing. I was afraid if I could finish my lunch soon. So, I was quick.

After the hour I skipped peon entered our classroom and said "Raghav, Father is calling you," my teacher said me to go. That moment I went cold, my hands and feet started to shiver as I was escorted by the peon to the Principal's room. I didn't know what was happening but many questions pelted in my mind. My loud voice became drab. I asked, "May I come in father?" "Yes", replied father. I rubbed my eyes and confirmed myself that they were Maggi's parents who sat opposite father. Father gave me a serious look and held his head. After some time, he took a deep breath. He asked me to grab the chair. I sat uncomfortably. I was panicked. Maggi's father was laughing at me. Father said, "Mr. Roy you only handle this issue." My mind began to question me. Heart was beating fast. There was a dead silence. Father came closer to me and gave a tight slap on my cheek. My cheek became red. He shouted on me for my deeds. "How dare you?" He asked, "Do you have Facebook account?" I replied, "Yes." He gave me another hit on my back. He asked, "Now tell me what have you done so far?" I answered him, "Father, I came to know that Maggi has no face book account. So, I created face book account with Maggi's name to talk with Anusha. I have been chatting with Anusha."

Later, Maggi and Anusha were called in. Father consoled both of them and asked, "Tell me what happened?" Maggi said, "Father, on Saturday, Anusha asked me, 'Yesterday, why didn't you log in?' She gave a puzzled expression and replied, 'I don't have any Facebook account.' I couldn't speak much about this with Anusha as the long bell buzzed." "Father, I went home and was shocked when I found an account on my name," my dad felt very bad about this fake account and went out to find the creator. After a moment, the two girls left as father asked them to leave.

A minute later, Father asked, “I want you to come with your parents, now go out and don't enter this building unless your parent is with you.” I licked my lips and was unable to sit, I moved ahead and asked, “Father, please forgive me. I am bad, please scold me”, I wept. I shook with sobs when Father wiped my tears and gave me a warm hug. He said, “Raghav, you are neither a kid nor an adult. It was just an attraction and you were attracted. You need to understand what is love. True Love stands the test of time. You don't have to give up on something to find it. If it is yours, it shall always remain. For now, your primary focus should be on education. If you are constructing a house you will have to wait for it be completed or live in it half done? So, you are a massive mansion, a place under construction. If you live in this half built structure, it may collapse at any time. Everything in life has a right time. Cheating can’t be tolerated anywhere. If you cheat in exams, you will be debarred. If you cheat in life, trust will no longer be with you. Anything and everything can be regained, but if character is lost it can never be regained. Hence, wait for the right time, presently you have to concentrate your studies. Don't be a disappointment to your parents and teachers. Love your parents and God. Surely, you will be rewarded. All the best”.

The Drag Of False Pride
(Pratiksha Karn)

I said, "I was not ready and now how would I handle this screwed situation? This has flipped my life to the next corner. It was my mistake that I didn't stood for myself but why didn't you all encouraged me? why you all went with the condition? Why hadn't you tried to handle the state?" An utter silence prevails. They both are into perplexity. With a few seconds delay Tara continues with a low voice, okay mom, I would be coming soon to meet you all, tell dad to take medicine on time and I am dying to see my love waiting there for me. "Yes, Tara take care", The call hangs up.

The clock strikes 4, how well we used to have gossips of our regular life near the lake. "This picture reminds me of everything. Sara and Diksha were so daring, how they used to flirt with the math's teacher, ah! This picture I captured on the college campus when they lost the game and they had to dance in the middle of the corridor", Tara giggles and murmurs to herself while arranging all the pictures. We were the spotlights of science section in our college. Apparently, they will also be missing those moments. Hugh! my stupid decision had placed me miles far from my happiness. living this life is worse than hell, I live because of my love, I am dying to see her, she grieves again.

The clock strikes 6, the door knocks and Aditya enters as usual with his usual grumpy mood. Within a minute delay in the evening snack, he rages loud at Tara, "You, stupid! What you do the whole day other than preparing food, you don't have anything to do still you are late for this!". "Oh! great, this if you told me a year before, I wouldn't be here with you. All that you made your fake standard in front of my family, this is what you are - a dependable being! and I am still with you just because of that one life whom you don't even care of. Seriously, I don't care about society's pressure anymore". Aditya and Tara continued their usual fight.

Next day, Tara with least will to see a new day, starts going through the job's recruitment section in the newspaper with a cup of coffee. "*Requirement of teachers in South zone, DPS*", the newspaper reads. "I wouldn't have stopped continuing my PhD course just for this sick life", she laments. She gets cranky and dumps the paper in the dustbin. Suddenly, a message pings on her mobile. She peeps and gets surprised by the message from Sara, "We are planning to join our school's reunion next week, you have to join us, Diksha is also coming, we will have fun seeing you there". They get extremely excited by the news of going to her place after a year. Her happiness was out of reach. She starts singing her favorite rock song and murmurs to herself how time changes. "There was a time when I craved to live in Mumbai, but now this is the most hated place to me. I am dying to see my love there; the only reason I bear everything. Yes, I will definitely go, my crazy friends will also be there yeah… nobody can stop going to Hazaribag, it carries a small place in map but holds my whole heart". "Ah! I am going to my home". Aditya can't see her happy face he dissuades her. "They will not remember you the same way, haha… Go I know you will come back here". "I am not asking you, I will go and that's done", Tara answers. "Then, go and don't dare to come back here, haha, now go… go…", he smirked. "Yes I will", she replied. Aditya and his mom shockingly heard her. "Her parents have not taught manners to her, so less dowry she brought from her home, I think Priyanka was than her son", Aditya's mom to Aditya. They mocked at her. Meanwhile, with tears in her eyes Tara leaves the house with her package.

Aditya has a dominating attitude just because of his job in a multinational company and a fair complexion. However, he and his family has stupid frame of mind. They believe in hiring a girl after marriage. For them a working girl, education of a girl or having a girl child are inferior. Their family prestige just lies on his son, Aditya's job, complexion and dominating attitude. Not only his family but there many families in North east who have this glass glory to brag about.

Within 6 hours of journey from Mumbai to Ranchi with a heavy heart and a worry of her dream to make a happy family is going to end. Her veins shivers with that thought, "what will be the condition next? What will happen to the little life? What will I respond to the society, they will question my character she mutters. A middle class small town educated or uneducated, a girl has to bear society's pressure in all means. Surprisingly, after reaching Ranchi airport, she gets welcomed by Sara and Diksha. A cute moment when three friends meet after 3 long years is out of the world feeling. The enigma is extremely different from any other thing. Within a fraction of second they burst into a loud psychiatric laugh. "So is our school's reunion the day after tomorrow isn't?" Tara asks in jest. "Yes, and so girls we have one day free, listen, nobody is going to say 'no' to my decision". Sara affirmed. "Wait, what? don't give your weird dares as you used to in college days, I am not going to confess my feelings to the math's teacher, Hugh", Diksha asserted. "Yes, yes, same here, no dare or do thing Sara", Tara continued. "My stupid girls, we have one complete day, let's enjoy to the fullest, let's bring back our college life, I have planned everything, booked the tickets too, lets rock in our own way girls", Sara said gingerly. "No, no Sara, I can't go I have to meet my family in Hazaribag, especially my love, you both enjoy", Tara said. "Sara is right, It's a great idea, you have to go with us Tara, you can't say no, yes Sara what's next?", Diksha continued. "Tara we will return just within a day, don't worry, as for now let's go to the pub, dance and drink", Sara tries to excite her. "Okay, girls, cheers to the moment, I want to live again, to smile real, to go far from this fake world, yes Sara I will go", Tara said cheerfully.

With the same smell of refreshment, the same vigor they enjoy that evening in the same pub dancing and clamoring in the latest rap song. Dancing all their hearts out.

"Sara is flirting with the dandies, she is still the same, where I am drifting to something very different", Tara to Diksha in envious way. "Tara, don't think too much; enjoy this second, mate, I am going to have one more shot". "These lights remind me of the darkness of my life, these loud songs haunt me of my silent existence", Tara to herself.

In spite of living in a small town, Hazaribag, these girls have modern living, however, all those modern methods are meant to be opposed in middle class society. It was only their educated upbringing and the present-day mentality of their parents which brought them much freedom in a good way. That teaches them to discriminate between right and wrong perfectly yet, they are from a middle class family, they have to suppress their decision about their life as their families' reputation in public have a greater position than anything else and they really live by that. The whole lot of the burden of reputation and status are much taken care of by middle class society which they are bound to maintain. In a judgmental circumference for only single gender in society, the three girls got enhanced education, where some parts of the town are still uneducated.

"Hurry up girls! We have to leave this place to our next destination, Tara take all those wine bottles in the car, Diksha, stop dancing and leave those shots, do not freeze my mind, go gather all my instruments, those speakers too, go! We are already late!", Sara hurried up. "Okay, okay, by the way where are we going?", Diksha asked. "There is no time to answer, come down, I and Tara shall be waiting in the car".

After 2 hours of journey with a mild song in the car and bumpy way, they move at 4 am by all the herky jerky pathway awakes Diksha in hustle "Hey, where are we now? Sara, I really don't want to get kidnapped by you laughs". "We are going to a hill station Netarhat, we will be reaching within an hour or three," Tara replies. "It is so exciting to plan a trip without letting anybody know Diksha utters in excitement.

The invigorating breeze of the hill enthralls them all, Tara was completely out of her mental strain, the air, the tall Sal trees put in heights of spirit within her. Each tor and shiny pebbles reminds her of vividity. Beautiful place, such beauty of nature, this smell of woods is far better than the engines of Mumbai, these chirps please me more than the unlimited beeping sound there in Mumbai. "Sara, look at those trees, isn't it distinct? Tara expresses". "These rolling hills are covered with sal, palash and mahua trees. The steep hill road (ghat road) cuts through the forests, runs some sharp bends, finally flattening into a plateau on which perches Netarhat at a height of 1,250 meters, amidst cypress and pine trees. This place is also called Queen of Chotanagpur and it is famous for the elegant view if sunrise and sunset", Sara explains.

"See girls it is cold, we have to walk a few kilometers after this, our car will not go up to the top, there are many rest houses, I have already booked the resting area until sunset", Sara says. "Let me remind you both that tomorrow is our school's reunion, we have to attend that too", Diksha replies. "Yes, of course, first enjoy this place", Sara responses.

The beauty of nature teaches many things in each step and right at the top, they saw the exact charm, the scene was overwhelming, they have never seen the rising sun this large and bright. The scent of palash and mahua entraps the place. Moreover, they rejoice the moment by playing music at their hotel room's balcony with sips of wine and a punch of snacks. After the sun sets, they shift into the yard and put on a bonfire, gulping glasses of wine they cheer that evening.

"You guys never know that I from a very young age earn for living for my family and myself and I know the power of money, one can dream, have wishes, have choices, can have goals only if one's pocket is strong otherwise all these are just fantasy in ashes. My only aim is to at least make an ordinary living for my sister and mother, after my dad passed away. I have been far away from this entertaining world for 3 years, that's why I planned a trip with my dear ones, Diksha and Tara, I really want my old amusing days back", Sara exhaled with grief. For the world she is a daring, fun loving girl but deep inside her soul has a deep stain of sorrow of unattainable goals and hardship of her living. A flicker of firmness overcomes the moment; the merriment of the moment now turns into the deep grounds that evening.

"Sara doesn't get delicate; you are a strength of our friendship. Life has different turns for different people. It has been 3 years since Siddharth left me, there's not a single day I haven't waited for, I have rejected all other proposals, I am love sick. Hence, I badly wanted my besties to jolly the way we used to", Diksha muttered. Each sip of wine now brings up the buried miseries, each snack continues with the crunch of their terrible life.

Tara with a sudden firmness added, "Our life has hitched, for me it is unbearable, family's goodwill, social status, some filthy agreements have made me so weak that I want to die. I am alive because of my cute little love, my 6-month old daughter. She is living in mum's house as her nurturing is meant to be a waste of time and money for her father, Aditya. My in-laws are greedy which I later understood, they proposed for the marriage just because of dowry. Although, they live in a metropolitan city, Mumbai yet they have a parochial mentality. I have come here for no hope to go back again. My married life has never been a happy one. I was fooled, Aditya had an affair with Priyanka, his colleague for 10 years, he can never forget her. Priyanka was liked by her whole family but her family was financially weak, her mother was a cancer patient. The reason he married me was the greed of money. These all I got to know after a year of our marriage when I had already conceived. His family mentally tortured me. And now I feel imprisoned by all the superficial norms of family and society. I never ever favored arranged marriages like this. He didn't even bother about his own daughter. I was forcibly living with him on the threat of getting divorced or more of social pressure. I don't know how my life, my marriage become a pretending dignity of this so called society, fake pride of in-laws, and the freaking necessity of myself to the relationship. They kept me as an unpaid servant. I left my studies, my job, my wishes just for serving him and his family as a servant, an educated servant. He used me just for physical needs. You all didn't know I had terrifying nights with him, when he just played with my body. How had I been so tolerant? My silence has maintained everything about the shallow prestige, the pseudo credit of both the families. I have tried to bear a lot only because of my daughter, thinking that things will change with a new life but some people can never change. He even refused to take the responsibilities, Friends and you know I had been in severe depression for the last 3 years, thank you Sara for organizing this trip I feel so light to share to my boon buddies".

Their Happy and thrilling time dispersed in regretful low spirits. But a glimpse of satisfaction was also held within them. They felt strong of themselves, because they three had different misadventures in life and they remained strong. Their roughness of life soothed by the new spirit of accepting and challenging the toughest condition, Next day they leave the place to Hazaribag, for attending reunion alumni at 11 AM.

"Rajveer, Harsh, Kartik, Shreyas; all are still good and unmarried", Sara utters in a cheesy way. "Yes, you are right, remember, everyone teased you with Rajveer's name", Tara replies. "Haha yes, yes, my eye is still on him, by the way where is Diksha?", Sara continues. "Look, she is with Siddharth, he has proposed to her right now, he remorse his behavior, they get happily back in relationship", Tara reports. "While you are busy flirting with juniors, all our batch mates are celebrating their patch up meantime, Kavita ma'am, Digvijay sir too".

"Tara who meets teachers in reunion, I don't want to ruin my time", Sara giggles and her phone rings "Oh! Just a second Tara, I will be back", Sara says. Within few minutes she comes back with a big smile on her face. "Taraaaa…, guess what… company's director ma'am has called me for my promotion Yay… she is impressed by my work and she hands over the executive office to me, I am so happy, let's celebrate Tara", Sara expressed her happiness.

Delighted, the reunion ends, everyone has different reasons of joy and indeed it fills bliss to them. However, there's still a feeble heart of Tara beating only for one reason. Tara reaches her home, "Sorry, mum I was rude in our last conversation, I am really sorry". "Ah, I understand, it was our mistake we prioritize our social status, we were mean to your feelings", Her mother responds. Suddenly an ear scothing giggling sound stopped their conversation. With claps and chuckles, the glittering eyes bring a trance to Tara. "No mum, if it was a mistake, I loved it, my child, I have been craving to see you", she weeps and hugs her tight. "Sambhavi, you are the only reason for my living, certainly I am blessed to have you, I will make your life beautiful, I will never pressurize you to go against your feelings, I will always understand you, I promise my child". After seeing her daughter, Sambhavi, all her messed up life seemed to be so fine. She gathers a unique strength. By a jovial tone Tara's dad asked, "Tara so when will you and Sambhavi go back to Aditya and live like a happy family?" Tara grinned and said, "never".

x-x-x-x

Tara refused to accept anything; those shallow relationships were now nothing to her. She rejects the false pride zone on such family agreements and making an obedient, never questioning daughter. All the tantrums of perfect stature, perfect living, perfect life partner, perfect education is burdened on a middle class society especially a girl given all the contemporary education but not the freedom to live by it. This mid-scale of society carries the false pride of being superior.

Finding Us
(Ritika Mahto)

There are times when we find ourselves at a place where we stand and try to discover ourselves.

"How good is to be great, but great work needs to be good."

It felt so casual to discuss something big.

Can it really be casual?

Like saying "hi" to all and smiling?

May be?

As time heals everything, I knew this time will cross similar

way.

To the ones who crossed the path, I believed I will also tread that way.

It's their part of life,

It was also that thought grew in my mind, is it that difficult?

Where knowledge seems less important and relatives' advices are valued more.

Which took years to acknowledge themselves?

It was their pain.

Their self hatred, which leads to give several advices.

Their regression, their unknown thoughts,

Yet they continued as if they are not affected.

True right?

Is it coming out? Or hiding behind it.

Still there are so many who hides their feelings in the name of – "what society will think?'

Afraid to be out to stand in front of the peoples who speak behind them not because they don't want to.

But because of their entanglements, their lots of engagements. The things that happened.

Made a stroll on their life, giggling, laughing and making stories behind. Which is not easily forgotten?

They never had a choice nor they choose to stay straight, But the same people who supported them say all have a choice and they should follow. Did we really see the truth or we hide it fearing and jump from the roof???

You should have shouted they say, and do not stand in front when we call them when away. And then what?

THE CYCLE CONTINUES TO ROLL DOWN THE STREET.

And what if we don't know it is something you should shouted at.

It keeps on going forgive yourself first...

It's painful yet it happened. May be its time we acknowledge it.

"The unfortunate thing about this world is that good habits are so much easier to give up than bad ones."

Nobody, but only she was hating him in extreme level. Not because of his gestures but because of his habit. Days passed and even the months when her sweet nature turned towards him.

They started dating after their final exam. He saw her in his college bus when they were leaving for their home. Sitting near the window seat she was holding her bag in her lap and the cold breeze that touched her skin and waved her hairs. Staring her cute face in school dress with two braids, her flawless skin glowed even more in the white uniform she wore. He was attracted at the first sight of those charming smile of hers and those gleaming black eyes which were chasing her friends while they were playing. Her baby hairs that fell all over her forehead kept the cuteness intact and that immature behavior of hers made him want to know more about her. Beauty is admired by all. So it was easier to extract the name of beautiful girls in the premise.

The Next day they happened to meet at college canteen for some formal discussion for event that was coming the next week. They hesitated while speaking but that made an eye contact between them.

Her cell phone gave her a notification. 'Arjun Kumar' sent you a friend request. She accepted it because the name seemed quite usual. And it started with texts, then calls and finally they started meeting and she didn't realize but he already took a special place in her heart.

"He wasn't good at expressing his feelings. But the days we spend together was no less than a dream for me", she explained.

She said "We dated for about 2 years but our relationship was very inconsistent. And now when I think about it, I feel like it was just one-sided love."

"So you mean you never loved him", I asked with curiosity.

"No. It's him who never loved me", she replied.

They would talk for about two months and he would vanish for another 2-3 months without any prior news. So there would be a communication gap for the next 2-3 months which eventually give her panic attacks. She would try to forget everything and move forward but he would come back again.

She was getting frustrated with what he was doing. But she can't stop herself from talking to him because she used to miss him badly in the days he wasn't there.

She thought at least she deserves an explanation. But their fights never had a conclusion because he never tried to resolve them. He would act as if nothing ever happened and would change the topic and try to be good at the present time.

"One fine day he received the call and blamed me for whatever happened in the past. She was brutally hurt. She still can't believe that he blamed her for something so precarious. And as she was already annoyed from his bizarre behavior, she started getting mood swings which turned her grumpy. She started being rude to everyone. She spoke harsh words. His behavior was affecting her mentally.

"It was doleful to see her during those days as those days were really tough for her. She almost lost her appetite. One of the most cheerful person in the group now became so grief-stricken", mentioned her roommate.

But her friends supported her. They took her for outings; spend more time with her so that her mind doesn't roll back to Arjun. It took time but slowly she started recovering that one day she came to know the reason for Arjun's weird behavior.

She could now connect every incident properly. He would be hallucinating and would be having trouble remembering stuff. He was having delusions. He was in his own world of dreams all this time.

"Our relationship never existed. All these days I was nowhere in his life. It was all fake", tears rolled down her eyes as she spoke.

"I don't know what type of person he really was. Sometimes he was really sweet and caring and sometimes I'm no one to him", she wept and moaned.

She continued, "I could sense different personalities but I couldn't recognize who is him. Those words that touched my heart. Did he really mean them? Or, he said them under the influence of a someone? He has been lying to me for all these days."

She finally decided to put an end to all this drama and she broke up. But the breakup had a terrible effect on him. Maybe he was hurt by the fact that she was no more with him or he had any other personal issues. But she really felt guilty by the step she took. She felt nasty and so she decided to take a step to help him out. She took him to the psychiatrist and started reminding him to take his medicines on time. When she felt that he was actually recovering she decided to move ahead in her life.

"I didn't have any grudges for him. So we parted our ways happily and decided to remain friends. Sometimes I do miss him but this was good for both of us cause losing a relationship hurts but losing yourself in a relationship hurts even more.", and she ended her story with a smile.

But love inside them was still alive.

She received a call on her 22nd birthday. "Wishing you a very happy birthday dear."

And I think that was the sweetest that brought a huge smile on her face and maybe that was going to last it for the entire day.

"I am in middle of something, I will call you back after I am done with my work"- Kritika said.

Winding up her work for the day, she rushed home thinking to call Arjun as early as possible.

"Phone rings"

"Arjun" calling displayed on her phone.

Taking a deep breath, she received the call with a smile.

"Sighs".

Are you tired? - "He Asked?"

"Yes", She replied.

"Umm- I wanted to say something to you.", Arjun said.

"Yes you can, what is there to hesitate", Kritika Said.

A little nervousness breaking his voice he started-

"*Let me take care of your broken heart*
and show you how to fly.
Let me hold you gently by the hand
Kiss your forehead and sit by your side.

Let me lead you to the sunrise
and out of needless rain,
'cause all I want right now
is to see you smile again.

Let me sing you all the songs I wrote
'til you sleep in my embrace,
and I'll keep you safe and warm until
the sunlight strokes your face.
Let me wake you up in my lap
and I'll let you touch the skies
to remind you of the strength I see

when I look into your eyes.

Let me kiss and show you what is love
and the happiness it brings.
You'll sail again like a butterfly
endowed with pretty wings.

Let me do all these to let you see
our fates are intertwined.
You're the accidental precious gem
I've waited so long to find.

Let's Cheers those good days we had
Let's sing and dance a while,
Forgiving all our faults of our past,
Make our present shine.

So fly with me, my beautiful heart.
It's time we leave the past.
I'm yours to keep, and you are mine.
We're finally home at last.
With this I want to wish you a very happy birthday beautiful."

Smiling on the other she thanked Arjun and their conversation went on.

Because Kritika was leaving the next day, she was also packing her bags and informed Arjun that she will going her hometown for couple of days.

Surprisingly, Arjun also mentioned about his journey, and said that he is also coming and asked her will she be joining the same train or not?

Listening to his statement Kritika said yes, and asked him to call her in the morning before he reaches to her place.

Excited and happy Kritika, packed her bag and set her alarm for the next morning because she did not want to miss this chance and also the train.

2nd February,

It was 4 am in the morning when Kritika woke up before her alarm rang. She rushed, fresh and up and got ready to leave for the railway station.

While she was on her way to railway station, many thoughts were running in her mind.

Maybe because she was excited to meet Arjun and that thought made butterfly flies in her mind.

Few minutes and I will be there soon – Kritika thinking on her mind.

As she reached the station she rushed to the ticket counter, seeing the long queue, she called Arjun asking him to help her out.

Rushing through the stairs, did not wanted to miss the train she called him and asked about the coach and the berth no.

Finding him she entered the gate. A little nervousness was there inside her and excitement too because she was going to meet him after years.

Tapped on head, called her and said where are you heading?

Smiling continuously, she set her luggage and sat down on the seat.

"Where is my gift?", Asked Kritika.

Kissing her cheeks – Arjun said, "For now I can only give this to you."

In 1hr journey to their hometown both smiled and saw each other. Thinking to start conversation, both just gave the stupid expression as if they were too shy to express their excitement.

Kritika started, "So, how have you been so long? I mean I was so excited to meet you and share all of the things with you. But then I was also thinking about your busy schedules and then I stopped texting you."

"Wait, wait, wait? How much do you speak? You are still the same, not even changed a bit.", Arjun said to Kritika.

"I will remain the same for you till last breath", Kritika replied.

Even after the incident that happened with them they were standing firmly with their positive thoughts and that made their relationship even more strong.

Sharing all the old memories of their life, they even forgot about the time and they reached their hometown.

"It's time we have to leave.", Kritika said after taking a deep breath.

"It's not the end yet Kritika, you already know about it. the best part is we are still good friends.", Arjun replied.

Trying to get him back she found him and leaving everything behind, they smiled and hugged each other and promised to meet soon.

It was not the ending of Arjun and Kritika's relation. They happily parted their way to home by finding each other once again.

It's true that relation once made cannot be broken easily because if it's meant to be it will happen.

Life Moves On
(Samir Kumar Mandal)

The Howrah Indore Shipra Express has not yet departed. "Some electrical fault is there" a tea hawker reluctantly told. One hour has passed. There is a protest going on outside- "CAA, NRC...". Co-passengers are taking 'this side' or 'that side'. 'Argumentative Indians' Sukanto yells. He looks outside. Asansol is the same as it was 15 years back. Nothing has changed here. Only his mother left him last year.

The Sun is almost in the middle of the sky; he can see from the door. A flock of birds is sitting on platform shade. Everything is going on as it was to go. On that unfortunate 24th May too, the moon was smiling in the sky without bothering his mother's funeral. Sukanto's eyes got filled with water.

He got the news early in the morning. His sister rang him up. His mother's health was not going well. The previous day, he talked to his mother. It is not that he was unaware but when the final news came, his knees could not stand, everything in front of his eyes became dark. He reached home in the middle of the night that day to do the last rites.

He walks down the memory lane. His mother was suffering from acute pancreatitis with sugar and thyroid problems. His father and sister did everything possible, but… Sukanto thinks it is not pancreatitis that has taken his mother's life, it is the tension of a mother for his son who lives 1000 miles away. Sukanto could not reach his mother's death bed. The guilt haunts him.

Sukanto opened his eyes. He did not realize that the train had started. It is running at a considerable high speed, but not like his mind though in the opposite direction. His mother was a simple village lady. She had not that much formal education but she was practical and human. When Sukanto could not do well in IIT-JEE, everyone in the family got perplexed, but it is his mother who convinced and persuaded all that life does not end after a single exam. Now, the chaotic sound of two passing trains took Sukanto to his real self.

Sukanto looked at the co-passengers. Their discussion point has taken a paradigm shift from political national debate to pretty house-old things – someone's daughter-in-law is not caring, someone's daughter has eloped, etc… Sukanto shows no interest in their discussion. He concentrates on the newspaper. One of the news draws his attention, "A high profile executive of a multinational company at the age of 40 years had suffered a massive cardiac arrest." Work Pressure, Family Tension or Lifestyle, even the reporter is confused, so is Sukanto. He was contemplating on the matter.

All of a certain, the train got stopped. "This is a small station. There is no stoppage here". Many people have gathered outside. Sukanto could not find out what had happened. He came out of the compartment. Everyone was rushing to the engine side. Sukanto did that too. After some time, he saw that a lady was lying on the railway track. This train had collided with the lady. A girl child was also seen near the lady. The white saree of the lady has become red with the stain of the blood. RPF has not yet reached. No one came forward to see whether the lady was still alive or not. Nobody was eager to know the condition of the girl child. Some people were interested to prove the case as suicide one, some were sure that it was an accident case. Sukanto somehow managed to reach the victim. Many people from the crowd asked him not to touch the body. They said that it was a police case. But, Sukanto did not listen to them. He checked the pulse. He felt the pulse. He shouted for help. He took the victim from the railway track to the platform. Other people took the girl child. It appeared to him that both are still alive. The police came. They arranged for the ambulance. The ambulance took the two victims to the hospital. The police thanked him. Now the announcement of his train he heard. It will start within 15 minutes. Sukanto washed his mouth and hands. He changed his clothes. He took his seat. The train started. Sukanto also started thinking, His sixth sense is telling that it is not an accident, it is a suicidal attempt. Why do people take such a desperate step? Was the lady a widow? He cannot remember. If not, where is her husband? She did not even think of her child? Who will be crying for her? Her mother, her father, her husband or her lover. A lot of questions without any probable right answer crowded his mind. For some time, the thought of his mother disappeared.

"So you are a situational leader now?" Uncle told from the adjacent seat. "Definitely not" Sukanto replied. "It is the driver of the train only. But I am not thinking that. I do not know if both the mother and the child will survive or not. Even if they survive, how society will treat them." Sukanto continued. Uncle said, "Life moves on. Whether you celebrate it or not. Suicide is not a solution." Sukanto disagreed, "where the right to live is a question mark, right to die should be there".

Uncle said, "Life is a very short journey. Have pleasure to continue that journey. Do not quarrel over small things - over TV channels, who will tie the mosquito net's string. Do not get angry over your son's small mischievous things. Pamper him to some extent. One day you will realize this. But then you will have nothing to do. Think of me. My only son was murdered by police during the Naxalite movement. He was brilliant but he also had the same 'beemari' to change society. My wife tried to find out the reason behind the death and the failure of the movement my son spearheaded. The path of her son might be wrong but not his intent. My wife too committed suicide as she had no answer. But I did not like living in the past. So, I enjoy life with my friends. I go on tour. Today I am going to Indore. I continue to do small celebrations with my friends. So, my dear Sukanto, please live your life. Think afresh. Give space to your son. Just guide him. He will not dishearten you. Don't carry workplace to home. Then he said, it is 11:30. Tomorrow morning again we can talk."

Uncle went to his seat. Sukanto was lying on the side lower seat. The words of uncle made him think. His mother, the lady, and her child flashed in his mind. His mother, like the uncle, used to say the same thing "God has given us only one life, we have to live. Try to remain happy". Sukanto wept into tears, he did not follow his mother's advice and neglected his family and son. He has to change himself. Today itself he tried to save someone's life. He took a deep breath, The Shipra Express runs ahead - moving from one station to another, as life goes on.

The Fight And The Flight
(Samridhi Khanna)

Deep inside my nerves, I was craving to show my admiration to him, but sadly neither I was able to do that, nor him. Children always look up to their parents for support and acceptance. But in this emerging virtual world, we all are connected to others more than our family members. People miles away might know more about us than what our parents do.

2 years ago, I left my hometown and moved to a new city in search of a job. I took my seat on the airplane and was ready for my new path in the new city. After the takeoff, when the plane took flight above the clouds, I glanced outside the window where I saw the sun and the moon together in one frame, but in reality, they were still miles apart from each other. The moon takes the light of the sun and reflects, but the sun remains unaware of it.

It reminded me about the distance between my father and me, which seems close and complementary, yet stringently far away. Daughters are more connected to their fathers; we must have heard this somewhere in our lives. The same rings true for me; I admire my father more than anything else. But it seems like an invisible wall is there between us which hinders the connection.

Back in my hometown, my father knew I was going away for a long time and who knew when I was going to come back. Yet, he wasn't able to utter anything but, "Do inform me if you need anything there." It was deep consideration, but with a hesitancy of expressing love.

Probably because of the generation gap or lack of communication, I never shared much with my parents, especially my father. So I decided to get relieved of this hesitation. I wanted to reveal to him that I'm not silly but I'm different. I wanted to express the affection I had for him which I was never able to show. While watching those clouds, the sun and the moon, I started writing…

"Dear father,

Our relationship is of father and daughter, but we never expressed our emotions, neither you nor me. Just like you, I feel silence is the solution to avoid my many problems but it is not the solution for everything, especially when it comes to relationships.

I'm your daughter and I got my silence from you. You can understand it better than anyone else can. It may be hard to believe for you that I'm writing this letter to you rather than calling you, but it's true it's me. I'm more than I act and now I want to disclose it to you even more. I want to break the bond of silence which exists between us."

I got so indulged in writing this letter that I forgot I was on the plane between some unfamiliar people. I was writing my suppressed emotions. My eyes were full of tears which were noticed by the old lady sitting beside me.

She asked me, "I can see your eyes are watery. Dear, what's the matter?"

I answered her, "Sometimes I feel either people around are not able to understand me or maybe I have the fear that I'll always be misunderstood."

The old lady- "Oh child, I must tell you something with my experience. This technology might let you make 1000 friends but, you can't talk to all open-heartedly, out of those you may talk to 100 and 60 will listen to you, and if you are lucky enough, only a few will be able to understand you. Ahh...our times were different. Youngsters may not like it now but according to me, it was a golden period".

Sometimes, unfamiliar people understand us better. I didn't know about her times but I nodded. Her words reminded me of a quote that came to my mind which I saw once on the web.

"There are some people who could hear you speak a thousand words and still not understand you and there are others who will understand without you even speaking a word." - UNKNOWN

In the meantime, the cabin crew served the airline meal and the old lady started munching upon it.

This time, I controlled my facial expressions and continued writing...

"Actually, this is not the first letter that I wrote to you, I wrote many letters but this one is the first that I posted. Whenever I felt that I was misunderstood or I wanted to say something to my parents, I always used to write it somewhere, just to get away with that load."

The air hostess asked me to stop writing and tie the seat belt as the plane was going to land in some time. I did as she asked and waited for the plane to land. Till now in that letter, I had written about my experiences and everything I wanted to share with him. Moreover, I enclosed a little poem in it that I gifted him once on his birthday. After writing all this, I was feeling way lighter. I was lost in my thoughts and suddenly I heard somebody vocalizing. It was that old lady beside me who was chanting something with her eyes closed, possibly because of the high speed of the aircraft.

Sometimes, these elderly people are annoying but cute at the same time. I feel their toothless smiles are priceless. Their wrinkled skin went through all the gracious and cruel waves of life. I was smitten by this notion,

"One old person is an Everest of experiences and lessons."

With increased turbulence, she started chanting faster and louder. She might be doing this for her mental strength and safety. In an instant, I felt like the same old lady was sitting inside my heart who was terrified of what's happening and what's going to happen next. I wasn't terrified about the landing, but about the mask which will be no more on my face. I realized, in all these years I got pretty comfortable with the mask that I carry on my identity. In the meantime, the aircraft landed.

The old lady was relieved but I wasn't.

After collecting my luggage at the airport, I took the taxi and anxiously concluded the letter further...

"I think everything happens for a reason and in some past months, I went from many ups and downs which disturbed me a lot, I lost my hope and spark to live, I was really sad but my behavior is always neutral and I never show what actually I'm going through. Writing is always easier for me than speaking. I hope this method might open some new ways to form the connection which existed between us, but because of the familiar fear, it wasn't seen much."

The letter was ready. I pasted the stamp on the cover which had the appropriate address. I asked my cab driver to stop near a letterbox. As the spot arrived, I got out of the cab and walked towards the letterbox with many doubts in the head.

I asked myself, "Why did it take me so long to express myself to my parents?"

An answer came from within,

"It wasn't the hesitation which stops, It's the fear or the fact that not everyone understands."

Suddenly my attention shifted from the word 'affection' to 'understanding'. I commenced the letter from conveying my feelings and somehow finished it by clarifying myself the way I am. Indirectly I was yearning for someone who could understand and accept me the way I perceive the world, which I did many times but results were mostly ambiguous.

I felt,

“No one is right or wrong,

It’s just the individuality

This should be respected by all.”

No matter how many times the moon revolves, it will never reach the sun. Repeating things won't make any difference unless the direction is right. I decided there’s no use explaining myself again and again if people who are listening to me, don't accept me the way I’m. I saw there were 2 boxes together in front of me, a dustbin and a letterbox. Ironically, both were going to do the same thing. My parents shall read the letter but eventually, they will remain the same as they were before.

I closed my eyes, took a deep breath and threw it in the dustbin instead. In the noise of vehicles on that busy road, I messaged my mom, “reached safely :)”.

“Fears and doubts took over.

The words were left unsaid.

The Flight was now over,

But the fight within was still on.”

Are You Still Alive?
(Sathiyapriya Suriyanarayanan)

Success is aspired by everyone. But humaneness is shared only by a few. It is not only human beings that expect benevolence, but all the living creatures in the world.

All the visitors of the Elephanta Caves crossed a little wounded monkey. Nobody seemed to care for that. The monkey was shouting in pain and expected help from anyone. But it was all in vain until Gowtham reached that place. The little monkey felt so happy even in pain when Gowtham embrace it in his hands. The little monkey was injured in leg and bleeding severely. Gowtham carefully handled it and tried to clean the wound. The little soul felt pampered like a baby and enjoyed that motherly care from a human being.

After few steps Priya realized that Gowtham is not following her. She turned back and shaken to found him standing in a place.

"Hey Gowtham! What are you doing there? We are running out of time. Come soon" she shouted from a hill-top. But Gowtham didn't turn. She was unsure whether her voice reached him. So she shouted again in loud voice. "Gowtham., Today is the last day of our expedition and we are left only with few hours. Come soon dear".

Gowtham turned deaf ears to her. He was busy nursing the monkey. Priya ran hurriedly from the top and noticed he is having a monkey in his hand.

"Hey Gowtham! Are you an Archaeologist or a Veterinarian?" mocked Priya.

"Come dear. Hold it in your hands. We should treat it immediately" Gowtham seeks Priya's hand in helping the monkey.

"Are you kidding? Leave it once and come with me."

"Priya… Understand. This little soul is bleeding."

"But Gowtham this is our last chance. Without entering this cave how will you finish off your research paper? Without the research paper how will you get nominated for the AIA award? This is your dream my dear."

Gowtham and Priya are Archaeologists. They are working together for five years and fell in love with each other. Gowtham's aim is to enroll himself in Archaeological Institute of America and to receive its Gold medal for distinguished Archaeological achievement. He has already done so many commendable research works and the expedition to the Elephanta Caves is an imperative one for him. Priya's endeavor is to help Gowtham in achieving it. Gowtham has promised his father the gold medal as his birthday gift the next year.

Gowtham lost his mother when he was at the age of 5. His father, being a single parent, devoted his entire life for him. He refused to re marry when the relatives insisted him. "My son is my world. I will be a good mother for him."

He loves his father and always wanted to make him proud. When Gowtham started his graduation his father was happy for him.

"I wanted you to become a successful man. You must achieve something in your life."

"Sure papa. I will definitely do that. Keep watching. One day I will make you proud."

"I am so happy for you my dear. God bless you."

Gowtham always recite the words of his father in his mind. When he became an archaeologist, his father felt proud of his son. But that was not enough for Gowtham. He wanted to make his father the happiest man in the world. When he came to know about the gold medal award from AIA, he made up his mind to receive it and dedicate it to his father as a surprise token of success. He worked hard for that for almost a year.

"Hey Gowtham, a happy news for you!" exclaimed Priya in joy.

"Yes my dear, tell me."

"Our last expedition of this year is to Mumbai. Your long awaited Elephanta Caves", screamed Priya in happiness.

"Wow! That's the happiest news you have brought today my dear. How many days are we going to be there?"

"It's just for a day dear", she answered in a low voice. "We didn't get the consent. Our officer tried a lot to get this one-day permission especially for us."

"It's okay dear. That one day is enough. I'll complete my research in an excellent way. Be my side. I will submit the paper within a week. Next award is waiting for my research paper", exclaimed Gowtham.

Priya knows very well that Gowtham was waiting for this opportunity for a long time. She was with him in all his thick and thin. So now she is taken aback to see him forgetting everything and wasting his time just for a monkey.

"Are you mad Gowtham? Are you going to spare your dreams just for this silly monkey?", she shouted in anger.

"This is also a living being Priya. Had it been a human being, will you just pass by? Definitely no. Why should we shun this little living being then? It will take just ten to fifteen minutes to save a life. That's it. I have given a first aid now. Let me surrender it to the security and I will join you", Gowtham took the monkey to the security officer and asked him to give the necessary treatment. The little monkey showed the gesture of gratitude. Gowtham felt really happy and with full content he joined Priya for the excavation.

"Let's go my dear. We are still left with three hours."

"But is that enough Gowtham?" questioned Priya in doubt.

"Let's make our best. Had I left the monkey unattended and entered the cave, definitely I wouldn't have concentrated. Who are we as human beings if we ignore the suffering of others? My father taught me to be the reason behind people's smile. Now I am satisfied. My dad will also feel happy for me if I share this to him" Gowtham shrugged his shoulders.

"I am so proud of you dear. People have become so selfish these days. Even I was also egotistic and rushed to my way without noticing the monkey. No one shows kindness in this modern world. 'Humanity' is taken off from the recent dictionaries. I thought humanity is dead. But now I realized that it is still alive and fresh in people like you. I love you Gowtham".

"Love you too dear".

They joined their hands together and entered the caves happily.

You must not lose faith in humanity. Humanity is an ocean; if a few drops of the ocean are dirty, the ocean does not become dirty. - Mahatma Gandhi.

My Perfectly Imperfect Life
(Sonali Mandal)

At 38, I started feeling miserable. "Why am I not enjoying my husband's company? Why couldn't I take care of my only son? Why are there sheets of dirt on my furniture and my favorite showpiece? Why don't I want to talk to my parents? Why am I on social media for long hours? What happened to my hobbies? Why am I oversleeping? Why would I cry secretly for pity matters? Where is my charming ever-smiling face? What has happened to my hair? Why is my skin so dry like never before? Am I going crazy?" I could understand that the demon has already grabbed my life like a virus and now began to cast its spell on me. The same demon, who made Shrivastav auntie's 27-year-old banker son to jump off the 6th floor to cuddle death.

So, in one monotonous evening, I gathered all my strength and fixed an appointment with a psychiatrist to get some oxygen to live until my son grows up and is able to take care of himself. And I spoke up, to my husband, I spoke clearly that I am not enjoying my life. It has become so tasteless.

And then the drama began. I realized that my husband and my parents were more anxious by the name of a psychiatrist itself. They thought how can someone from their family be mad? But I didn't cancel my appointment because some kind of emptiness was eating away all my strengths and purpose of life.

At AIIMS, I reached before time and had to wait after the initial registration process. I prayed to God hard about two things, one I should not meet any known people and answer any obvious questions, two is that my doctor should not ask me too many questions. Yes, I was lucky as nothing of that sort happened on that day.

In the waiting room, I was surprised to see all normal people just like me except one or two with noticeably worn behavior.

Then as my turn came, I greeted the doctor and went inside. He asked me a few general questions like what may be the cause of my prolonged unhappiness, my chores, how much time am I able to spend with my husband, how long I was feeling lonely, if I felt like crying etc. Then he prescribed me medicine and said it's safe with just a bit of gastric discomfort. And asked me to follow up after a month.

The real adventure happened while returning home at the bus stop as I was waiting, I saw an elderly man wearing a suit fully engaged with a mobile phone. Sometimes he was laughing freely. He looked at me several times then he concentrated on his mobile again. After some time, the gentleman lifted his face with high power glasses and looked at me and asked whether everything was ok with my child. He seemed to be a teacher or a professor, a certain personality was being expressed in his whole body language. He asked whether I would like to have tea from the nearby tea stall, I agreed and both of us sat down to have tea, as we sipped tea I asked, common questions like "Where are you from? How many children? What are they doing?" The gentleman said that he was a professor at Calcutta University. For a while, both of us were quiet. The gentleman asked in a quiet voice, "How do you like the taste of life? Are you having a good time at home?" First, I couldn't figure out what to say. The gentleman said to me "Are you enjoying the sweetness of life? I want to know if there is enough sunshine in life?" I smiled and said, "At eight o'clock in the morning my husband goes to the office and then comes back eight at night. The rest of the time is either I have trouble with myself or me and my son, actually most of the time with my son… Why wake up late in the morning, why not do homework? Why did he leave food in the dish? Why didn't he pack his school bag? Why is the bedsheet so crumpled? Why are books not in place? Why did he get up on the couch without washing his feet? How much TV or computer will he watch? etc. There is nothing in my control. Sometimes the mood is so pissed off that I feel lost."

The gentleman took a short sigh and said, "This is the most beautiful time of life… Don't neglect it… Drink this elixir of life to the fullest engrossing all your senses enjoy it".

"There will come a time when you come into the room and see the silence around the room, the bedsheet would always be pulled up tightly, the day-to-day conflict between you and your son ending in a miraculous gesture will no longer be there, you will miss the impromptu battle with your husband… There will be dust-coated lining on the books… you will feel like spreading books again on the clear table and help your son with his unfinished homework holding his hand. Everything will be fine but the loneliness of the desert all around, just wandering around in the hope of getting the child's familiar smell once, no one will wave goodbye with little hands. The TV will continue on its own no one watching it mindfully, there will not be any argument over the remote., The food will keep drying on the table no one will ever sneak the egg yolks out the hard-boiled eggs, the sweet voice of your beloved son on mobile will keep reducing from every day to weeks. And a week to every month, then every two months. He will come for two days; he will carry with him all your dreams in his baggage. The power of hearing and sight will be more nimble. Insomnia will have stronger roots to make the nights longer."

The gentleman's words were like an arrow that shot me right in my heart. The loud horn of the bus startled me. We boarded the bus and luckily got a seat beside the gentleman I said, "then what is the right way to live?" The gentleman, with a bit of a sore throat said "Don't be like a withered leaf, be like a few green leaves in an old tree. So good old friends can be the ray of sunshine you need to extinguish the fire of loneliness and provide warmth to the whole of your body. Only a friend can indulge in the fountain of endless laughter in your lost life, that's why I kept the little window open on that mobile. A word of an old friend flashing in could be like a ray of sunshine in your blues. Be careful to keep the old friendship. Losing in today's day-to-day work is a shadow of their friendship." "I am going to meet our friends today at the ceremony. Every three months we meet in different parts of the country." "After two days of drowning in the noise of music, playing, laughter. I can find the oxygen of survival." "We do not know what our future will be after 20 years? I do not know whether I will be able to type on the mobile or not? Maybe the eyesight will slowly blur… The group members may not be able to sing or dance. My hearing power may cease slowly; my memory will be blocked. But the friendship never stops…"

"I got down at my stop with a new dimension in my life".

Meera – The Girl Of New Era

(Sri Harshika Gudlavilleti)

It was raining cats and dogs!! It was the north-east monsoon season which tends to bring about torrential rains in and around Chennai. In the busiest part of Velachery region of Chennai, lies the serene Blossom Apartments that houses large number of nuclear families. With both the parents usually out on work, it is every evening routine that, all the children of Blossom Apartments assemble near Pattiyamma for a story session. Mr. Ravi's mother and Shilpa's grandmother, Kousalya is regarded as Pattiyamma by the entire children gang of the apartments.

Today, being a Sunday evening, once again all the children assembled in Shilpa's house for another story session by her granny. However, the moment they saw that Pattiyamma was seriously immersed in going through that day's newspaper, the frown on her forehead was telling them something else!!! Kids felt she was not in a mood for story telling today!!!

"Patti seems to be so disturbed today!" said Vishal in a sad tone, afraid that he may not get to hear a story today! "Okay Patti, we are leaving for today" said another child from the group of kids slowly filling Patti Amma's living area. As all of them started their way back home seemingly quite disappointed, they get to hear Patti Amma's voice ordering everyone to sit down. In her melancholic voice, she then said "Today the story is going to be something that you will enjoy and something that you will find knowledge out of!". She continued, "This is something related to the news that we are getting to hear very often, these days!". From the audience came out a small voice - "Is it about that movie actor, Patti??" "No! Listen to the story very carefully as this one is unlike any other stories" replied Patti.

And it goes thus…

"This story is about two young siblings, Riya and Niya, who live in a slum area of Mumbai. It was during one of the busy days of their lives, that Riya shouts out for her younger sister - "Niya! where are you?? The school gates will shut the moment clock strikes 8!!!" "Ok! Ok Tayee!" said Riya in an irritated tone. They both are hardworking and always aim to reach sky and want to become rich so as to fulfill all their and their family's dreams. Niya is always a tad lazier than Riya and it is always Riya who keeps covering up for her younger sister, in times of need. They started walking fast, towards their school in the neighborhood.

Riya and Niya are studying in classes 10th and 8th in the local government school and are quite known for their ambitious and studious nature. They always volunteer for any sport or event of their school and are quite loved by their school teachers and students alike.

On the other hand, Maya and Meera are two other siblings who reside in the adjacent gated community, 'La Parele'. They both are so industrious, simple and kind hearted. They also have high ambitions like Niya and Riya. They want to get their jobs by their hard work and use their skills to make up their name in today's world but not by using anyone's influence or their money.

On a similar day, in Maya's house, Maya is talking to her younger sibling, Meera - "Ahh! It's so cool!! Meera, please switch off the AC dear!". "Ok di! But first tell me did you complete your social project?? And did you complete reading 'Sudha Murthy's book's summary for your 'Social Skills' school work?", said Meera. "Oh! There is still one more chapter left Meera! what shall I do now???" Maya replied with a sad note in her voice and face, both! Here Meera is always the go-getter and seems to be a risk manager for Maya. "I knew you wouldn't complete it! That is why I kept all the references ready on the study table. Check it and write the matter in your social project and I have highlighted the important paras in the book – "The

Day I Stopped Drinking Milk". Please go through it once. It might give you an idea of coming up with a summary for the event today!", Meera said as a matter of fact. "Oh Meera!! You are such a darling!! I knew I can always count on you, my dear little sister!!', exclaimed Maya.

Maya and Meera study in an International School setup in the premises of La Parele, in classes 10th and 9th respectively. As part of their curriculum, they need to visit the government schools and hold an event where they can discuss and interact with each other and help the weaker students with tips and tricks to improve their academics and other social skills.

Today, they are supposed to visit the same government school in which Riya and Niya are studying, to conduct the social interaction event. As soon as Maya and Meera, along with their fellow students, reached Riya's school, all the four girls instantly hit off the ground. The leadership qualities of Riya and Meera helped each other in controlling the crowd and conducting the event successfully. Niya and Maya helped their siblings eagerly in the event and also made new friends amongst the other school children.

Soon after the event, it became a practice for all the four girls to meet every weekend in the play area of the apartments and the highly educated parents of Maya and Meera also did not object this new friendship of the little girls. Since both of Maya and Meera are working parents, they make sure that their girls are in safe hands and are aware of things like 'Good Touch-Bad Touch', 'Self-defense' and other techniques to protect themselves independently.

On one such weekend, Riya and Niya, as usual visited La Parele campus grounds and while all the four girls got busy playing hide and seek in the park, except for Niya, all the other three girls could be found out. Riya, Maya and Meera frantically started searching for Niya, but, without any success!! Slowly, the evening light started fading into clouds of darkness and the visibility too started thinning. Riya started crying and blaming herself for being careless about her young sister. Maya started coaxing her while Meera prepared everyone to go in search of Niya, without wasting any time further. She alerted the security personnel and also a few more elders who were eager to help the girls in searching for the missing girl.

She collected all her friends from the housing complex and divided them into groups and sent them in different directions. La Parele being a vast expanse of gardens, play area, swimming pool and other amenities, there was a risk of the search party also to get misguided. Hence, she made sure that they will leave a sign as they proceed in the path, so as to follow back into the central part of the garden, where they are to assemble within a few minutes and share their findings. The entire exercise was done on a war-footing and in the meanwhile she made sure she informed her parents, who in turn informed the local police.

Soon, the entire garden and play area of the La Parele housing community is converted into a war-zone where each of the participants is busy finding out and sharing any minutest detail of the missing girl. Maya is put in charge of handling Riya and also trying to inform Riya's parents about the whole incident.

Suddenly, at around 8 pm, someone in the crowd comes up with a small purse and someone else, with a slipper that were scattered in the remote part of the garden. Riya has a look at them and immediately screams out her sister's name, confirming that they belonged to the lost girl, Niya.

Now, Meera takes it upon herself to go to the place where these items were found and starts searching for further clues. She soon comes across a red ribbon that she remembers having seen on Niya's plaits. Under the glow of the garden lights, she puts all her energies to search for any small clue that can help her find Niya. She soon comes to the swimming pool situated in the remote corner of the Society. Near the staircase going into the pool, she sees something glittering and realizes it to be a small silver pendant in the form of letter – 'N'. As she looks about her, she sees something floating on the water in the pool, which looks like a silver chain. Immediately, she runs back to the place where all were supposed to be gathering. Meanwhile, Meera's parents also reach back home along with the local police constables.

Meera shows all the pieces of clues to Maya and Riya who recognize all of them as the belongings of Niya herself. Meera rushes the elders to the swimming pool and shows them the floating chain.

Immediately, the elders in the group jump into the pool and start searching for Niya. Soon, they come across Niya who has become unconscious and has been almost reaching a point of breathlessness, drowning in the water. They pull her out and Meera immediately starts giving her breath through her mouth. Soon, Niya was resurrected back and comes to senses. Upon refreshing, she mentions that when she was searching for a place to hide during the game, she was inquisitively looking into the pool, when she felt a sudden push from behind and she fell into the water after which she lost her senses.

Now Meera takes it upon herself to find out as to who it was, that pushed Niya into the pool. She starts questioning each of the crowd present around and suddenly points at a boy of age around 15 years and shouts – 'Raman! I know it is you who has pushed Niya into the water. Isn't it?'. The boy, Raman starts stammering and denying his involvement. However, people soon come to understand it is Raman himself who has done this gruesome deed, by the sheer look on his face!!

People then start questioning her on how she could find out that it was Raman. She tells them that, "The first time I met Riya and Niya I happened to meet them by solving their fight with Raman. Even after that, Raman was always teasing or rather started bullying Niya for he, couldn't bear the insult caused by Niya in school. I remember, once Riya had told me that he was speaking vulgarly and is a thief who was stealing things from Niya's class so, Niya complained on him to the principal. Also, he could barely digest the fact that Niya is always class topper, and is unable to beat her up in the exams. With all this jealousy, he had come into this extent of trying to kill Niya. So, when I gathered all the information while searching for her, I could only see Raman on top of it! Here when I saw him sweating, tensed and also he was about to run from the scene so I could easily identify him as the suspect!!!!"

All the elders in the group reprimanded Raman and the police constables took Raman along with them to the police station, for further questioning.

Now, in the present day, Pattiyamma addressed the group of children in her home – "So kids, do you know what happened next?? Yes, you are right! Meera was given a loud applause for using her knowledge and intelligence in the right time!!! Later Niya's parents, Riya and Niya thanked her a lot for saving Niya's life. And, Raman regretted himself for doing such a bad thing.

"So, that was today's story did you like it kids??" all the children together shouted – "We loved it Patti Amma. We learnt a lot from the story today!! Especially from Meera!. We will also try to be so alert and as quick-witted as Meera!! Your stories are wonderful!! You make every story a movie experience! Waiting for your next story Patti! Meet you tomorrow bye!!"

Saying so, all the children scurried away back to their homes, as the rainfall receded and their tummies and brains were satisfactorily filled with home-made hot jalebis and samosas served by Pattiyamma along with the scrumptious story!!!

Dimly Lit
(Sukriti Bansal)

She stood there in the darkness, where even her light could not get a glimpse of her. Demeaned by her own thoughts, will he? Or will he not? She asked herself. She was deciding over something even the world couldn't help her in.

"Ami says Allah Talla loves his children, will he not allow me?" she said to herself out loud.

Sitting in a closed room, dimly lit, after reading her *namaz* with a pure heart, she bowed in *sajda*, and then after a while completely lost track of time and let her unconscious self-take over, she couldn't stop but think about the lover she wants in life, will Allah never let her be his if he's not of the same religion, she did not get up even after her legs got stiff after *Qidah* position she was sitting in. It was her mother's voice that brought her back to the realm of Allah and Quraan.

She thought to herself if Allah can ever permit her to *sajdah* in front of the man she has been dreaming about, or will 'he' ever enjoy her *aayat* that she will dedicate to 'him'.

"Yes, Ami!" she could not think about anything but the lover she could not name in the proper Muslim family. She was scared to tell about her intensions to the member who would just cut her off with the first word she murmurs about him.

With this thought the sun held together its rays and went back to its hiding place. Even the moon seemed to tease her as she sat in her room; a room with just one bulb, which seems to flicker on a very odd moment, an old fashioned cupboard was put on one corner and a side table to one. It was a very small room which could have had only space for one person to stand after putting bed in the middle.

Shahista was very slim so she could get in the spaces where no one could even think about going. She looked at the moon that hid behind the clouds to tease her mind, she could feel moon's gaze on her light skin. But it disappeared after every five minute because maybe it was in a mood to play 'hard to get'. With that she realized neither she is lit nor burnt, she was dimly lit in this vast city, and doesn't really know what she wants but the question was will she ever be able to find it.

The next morning, she woke with *Fajr*, she lived in Nizamuddin East, an area where after *Fajr*, all one could hear were the noises of traffic and horns, that she got habituated to with time. It was the vacations after completing her 12th, her *ammi* used to pray to Allah Talla every day, that her daughter gets admission in one of the best colleges around so that she could get her family out of their debts and this dirt.

"Ami… I' m going with my friend Khushi for a while; I'll be home in an hour. We are going to buy some college forms". Shashista heard her voice echoing in her ears; she knew she could not wait any longer. She threw some perfume on that her uncle got her from Dubai, that she kept for some special occasions and she predominantly used it when she wanted to see his face.

"Why do you always have to go out with that Hindu girl? Can't you take Reshma along, you know if you father gets to know about this inter religious friendship how will he react"

Shahista rolled her eyes and said to herself, "They can't accept Khushi, how will they accept you?"

"Ami I am leaving, will be back soon", said and closed the old wooden door behind her.

She wore the anklet that made merry sound to distract him or to lure maybe, she didn't know how to do makeup like the other girls around but with her old fashioned thoughts she smiled and giggled like a 12-year-old.

She was 17, ready to go to college and spread her wings. She could feel the December chills in the scorching heat of July, she could feel the gush of wind playing with her hair and she thought of him even more.

"Will he like my hair in a bun? It's okay. I will open it if he doesn't".

"Will he like you?" she questioned the anklet, and then smiled on her own thinking about the answer as the anklet seem to smile with her with their tinkling sound.

She walked fast so that no one asks her about her purpose and also she didn't want to get late for the *aarti*. As he promised her, he'll meet her today in the temple nearby her house, secularism is a great ideal that can be found everywhere on the streets of Delhi.

She saw the *paan wale bhaiya* on her that gives complementary *paans* to her father; she wished she wore her *burqa* today. As if anyone saw her entering the temple rather than mosque it could have raised a number of questions and swords in the name of practicing Delhi's way. And she knew she will be the first one to be chopped off and how another issue will rise to a height as Babri masjid.

She lowered her face and walked away.

And coincidently she bumped into aunty Yazmeen, who likes to gossip more than keeping her family happy.

"As-salam 'alakyum" she said in her scoffing voice and cocky smile" her hairs were as red as the view at dawn and her teeth as orange as sun giving it in.

"Wa alaykumu as-salam" said Shahista with a frozen look at her face as if chills wrecked her spine and her hands couldn't even move to promote the gesture of her words anymore.

Asking people where they were going is a bad omen but aunty Yazmeen was as bitchy as ever. She threw a frown at Shahista's face and asked "*Beta* where are you going?" Shahista with a heavy heart said "I am going to collect some forms".

Aunty Yazmeen threw the comment as always and said "what will you do studying, I have a suitable boy for you, if you know what I mean. It is such a tender age and before you know you are ripped and rotten for no good man".

Shahista gave a smug smile and said "I would rather hold my degree till 21 than a baby but thank you for such a delightful offer."

She snubbed aunty Yazmeen and walked away and gave a sigh a relief. She hid her face even more carefully, she walked even faster. Felt like she could not get hold of her breath. She could hear the bell ringing, and felt like her anklet made conversations with the sounds around or of the bell.

She reached the temple, and walked up the steps taking the name of her beloved secretly.

She reached up to the ideals and rang the bell that will let her beloved know of her presence but maybe he already knew about her arrival, as she entered the temple a cold breeze took over her mind, it became a balmy day due to that breeze.

She saw him and everything seized. She walked with a low pace but still couldn't catch her breath, felt like she was huffing and puffing. Her heart rate was at pinnacle; thought she might just pass away right now. She did not even want to blink; it made her think of losing even seconds of his face.

"I came for you. You like my yellow suit, right? And what about the anklet?" She smiled with his sight; he looked as beautiful as ever. Holding flowers in one hand and…and…

She could not stop smiling.

He was the one who stood there with a flute in his hand and a peacock feather in his crown, the one who wore yellow clothes all the time, the one who is known as Krishna by the world. He was her beloved, she enjoyed how people celebrated him and he could tear down all the walls, even of groups that people have made. He was the one who would cherish every *aayat*, every holy word from Muslim *pak* world and would never judge her.

He was her *Kanha.*

Believe It Or Not
(Vaishnavi Sistla)

Today at school I had a fight with my classmate who is also my neighbour. Actually I was talking to someone else and had not heard her. She felt that I had not answered her on purpose. She misunderstood me and reported to our teacher about the same. So I decided not to talk to her. I was walking home all by myself after school, thinking about what had happened earlier that day. On the way I twisted my ankle. The pain was horrible; I couldn't walk any further. So I sat down under the shade of a tree, to let the pain subside. Due to the cool breeze I fell asleep.

After a while, I woke up to the sound of tinkling voices. I saw beside me, tiny creatures with wings, dressed in pretty frocks. It didn't take me long to realize that they were fairies. They were so lovely that, all I could do was stare at them. Then one of the fairies spoke to me, I could hardly believe it. "I am Bella and this is my bestie Violet. We are fairies who live in this enchanted world along with many other magical creatures. You are sitting by our tree." It was only then that I realized the road that I had been walking on had vanished and I was amidst many trees with funny beautiful houses on, in and around them.

When I turned to ask Violet and Bella how I had ended up there, few more fairies and pixies had joined the group. I introduced myself to them "Hi! I am Vaishnavi." and then told them what I had been wondering. One of their friends asked "Do you believe in fairyland, fairies and the enchanted world?" I said "Yes". This was true and I had longed to meet the folk of the enchanted world. Another of them said "That's it! That is what has brought you to our land. By the way I am Rosy and they are Rocky and Rover." All of them were kind, sweet and so good at heart. I warmed to them.

Suddenly the sky turned dark and it got windy. I was puzzled because just a minute ago, the weather was so calm and pleasant. Everyone started fleeing to their houses. Bella gave me something similar to a jelly and asked me to gobble it. I did so. I felt as if I was shrinking and I really was. Within the blink of an eye, I was about their height!

Violet dragged me to her house which was on the ground. As soon as we were inside she heaved a sigh of relief. It was warm and cozy there. She looked at my puzzled face and began to narrate what had happened. "Until a few years ago, everything was fine and everyone in the enchanted world was happy. Our king Gold and queen Sparkle ruled our world wisely and justly. Then came the D-Day. There was a ball at the palace that evening, all of us were heading to the castle. Quite suddenly everyone started running and screaming for help. I noticed Witch Wicked fly across the sky with her wand. On seeing her I too ran for my life. Eons ago Witch Wicked was put into prison for trying to poison the queen. That day she had freed herself from the prison and turned our kind king and queen into lifeless statues and declared herself queen. From then on, this terrible sate has dawned over us." she ended sadly. "She has not spared any being who came in her way. The weather always changes from good to bad when she arrives. We rush to our houses to be safe."

I was astounded. I had always imagined the fairy land to be a splendiferous place. I never thought that it would see bad times too. I pulled myself together quickly and spoke to Violet "Surely, there must be a way to solve it. You are not going to suffer like this forever?" She kept quiet and didn't answer me for a while. "Come on, there has to be a way out of this. Can she cast spells without her wand? What are her loop holes? Is there anything that she fears?" I asked, unable to bear the silent communion anymore. She looked at me with sparkling eyes. I guessed she had hit on something but couldn't guess what.

"I do know a way but let us go to Bella's before we talk about it" said Violet. "Do you mean to say that we are to go out into the darkness with Witch Wicked out there? I am certainly not stepping out of your house." I said firmly. Violet laughed at my firmly set face and said "Me too! I didn't mean that way. Come with me." I followed her into her bedroom perplexed. If she didn't mean going out of the house, what could she mean when she said "Let us go to Bella's."

We came to a trap door beside her bed. "Do you happen to have a torch?" she asked. "Mine has run out of battery." "I don't have a torch but I have a pen that gives out light. Will that do?" I said. I took out a pen from my pocket and showed it to her. "That will do" she said and took it. She led the way into a dark hole. The path was actually from inside the tree. Bella's house was on the tree. When we reached the house we saw that the others were there too.

As soon as Violet made sure that all the doors were closed, she started sharing her idea "Do you remember guys. Last time when Witch Wicked attacked the palace, there was a lot of wind and her wand slipped out of her hand and almost within seconds she too fell. So I feel if we can destroy the wand, we can weaken her and break her spells. Then Rover spoke "Yes you are right Vi but I have heard that she has a necklace which draws the wand to her and there is no chance that she can lose it." "Then we will have to first destroy her necklace." said Rocky. "Guys, I think few of us should ruin the necklace while the others steel her wand and shatter it." said Bella. "I agree with you Bella but let us get the necklace first then our job will be easier as the wand is drawn to the necklace." I said and everyone agreed to it. "Rosy, Rocky and myself will get the necklace and the rest of you take care of the wand while we distract her." I said. Then Rover spoke "Vaishnavi you have to keep her engaged while we rob the necklace from her." "Right. Are the rest of you ready with your plan?" I asked "Yes. You go ahead Vaishnavi" said Violet.

Though I felt nervous, I went to Violet's front door and opened it. At once Witch Wicked was in front of me. She entered the house and settled on a sofa and put her wand down. I was scared stiff but spoke courageously. Just as I was about to speak, Witch Wicked intervened "Ah! A human! I sensed there was one. Tell me how are people in your world." "Now a day many people are selfish and cruel minded "I replied truthfully. "Then my spells are working marvelously." she said. "What!" I blurted out before I could stop myself. Surprisingly she was pleased with my reply and spoke in a sickly sweet tone "People don't call me Witch Wicked for nothing. I am the one who controls the bad in all the worlds that exist, including your human world." "Was it due to this pest of a witch that humans were behaving so meanly?" I mused.

Meanwhile my friends were doing their job. Rocky had loosened the hook of the necklace and Rosy had very carefully removed the necklace out of the witch's neck while she was busy boasting. The very next moment Bella had the wand and threw it on the floor Violet and Rover were helping her turn the bad black magic into a good one. We didn't hear the crash of the wand as I sneezed very loudly just then, startling the witch. Light seeped through the window. The spell was lifting! The witch was fading and eventually disappeared into the air.

Everyone started shouting in joy. Rosy then gave me a ring which she had weaved from the lush green grass of the enchanted world. Bella said "You can visit us whenever you want, if you have this ring." Once you put it on, you will shrink to our size automatically" added Rocky. I smiled gleefully. Just then I felt someone shaking me badly. I sat up straight. It was my sister shaking me and I was in my room. "Get ready, you sleepy head. Come downstairs for breakfast. If you don't hurry, there won't be any left for you" she yelled and went out of the room. I was baffled. I couldn't believe that I was dreaming all this while for it had been so real. I remembered the ring and searched for it. I couldn't find it. So it had been a dream after all!!!

It felt different somehow as I went downstairs. I looked out of my window, managed to smile at my neighbour cum friend whom I had detested. Surprisingly she smiled back. There was this vibe of kindness, happiness and positivity flowing in me. May be I just explored the thoughts running through my mind last night and not the enchanted world ...the fairies and pixies were the good within me and witch wicked the bad part of me. I guess I felt positive not because I helped to defeat Witch Wicked in the enchanted world but because I helped myself to defeat the Witch Wicked in me. I wonder what a better place this world would be if everyone defeated the Witch Wicked within them and helped the good fairies win instead of trying to defeat others. With my experience I can say it is not too difficult… believe it or not!!!

KNOW YOUR AUTHORS

Adwika Tamrakar

Adwika Tamrakar is a 10-year-old girl currently studying in grade 5th.

She lives in Bengaluru.

Adwika loves to read and write. She enjoys action, adventure, comedy and fantasy.

She mostly writes fantasy and she is active on Wattpad and Quotev.

She is also learning the Keyboard and loves to play soccer.

Anjali Jha

Anjali Jha is from a small village of Darbhanga district of Bihar. She was born on 30th September 1997. She is pursuing B.Sc. (Horticulture) from Nalanda College of Horticulture Noorsarai from Bihar Agricultural University, Bhagalpur.

Apart from being a student, she is an avid reader, writer, poet, reviewer and blogger. Her works got published in more than 90 anthologies along with her 6 eBooks. Recently she has published her debut Hindi novel "Ek Pyaar Aisa Bhi".

She loves to play with words and write from the depth of her heart. She always expresses her emotions through words rather than sayings. She generally writes about love, relationship, emotions, pain and abstract. Writing helps her to survive in her worst phase of life. Writing is just like breathing to her because when she feels depress, she used to write her feelings. She is a dedicated but unpredictable personality, surreal in the way she holds her priorities, and realistic towards her goals.

Contact her :-
Facebook :- Anjali Jha
Instagram :- anjalikumarijha
Twitter:- AnjaliJha
LinkedIn :- Anjali Jha

Ankita Saloni

A 20 years old Ambivert Bibliophile who finds herself a perfect blend of sugar, spice and everything nice. Being an author, writer, poet, blogger, theatre artist and programming enthusiast, she loves to explore all dimensions of her interests and keeps on looking for various online and offline platforms to exhibit her talent. An art lover by heart, she is a person who loves experimenting with words, themes and genres to create something magical out of them. Being an avid reader of classics, she seeks solace in books and wishes to embark on a new journey every day, believing that only the sky is the limit for her.

Anshika Kodukula

Anshika Kodukula is an avid reader of mysterious and adventurous novels. She is a huge fan of Charlie Chaplin. She amuses all her friends. She keeps talking with all her mates without a single cessation whenever she finds some. She loves travelling to far off places and is a very big foodie. She is a travel photographer. Adventure, as mentioned above, is one more activity she is fascinated to.

Anshika was born in Rourkela, Odisha. She has resided in Hyderabad till she was 9 and is living in Vijayawada currently. She is a student of class 8 at Slate-The School which believes in the moto "Holistic, Realistic and Futuristic". She writes articles for the Times of India. Her parents, Kiran and Sudha, are very supportive and encourage her that, attempt itself is a very big win! Her English teacher, Mr. Feroz, had recognized the hidden talent and brought her up with flying colors. She looks up to Sudha Murty and Ruskin Bond. She is a proud SLATER.

Avijit Roy

Born in West Bengal Avijit Roy is a teacher by profession and writer and painter by passion. At present he is a teacher at a high school in his native state.

He is the winner of "South Asian Literati Award" organised by Dastaan (Pakistan) and "75 Rising Star Award" 2019 organised by Literoma.

His stories and poems have been published both in national magazines like Indus Women Writing, Indian Ruminations and international magazines like WINK (USA), Brilliant Flash Fiction (Ireland) and Broken Rule Publishing (USA).

His published books are "Children of a Whimsical God", "Sela, The River Princess", "A Sunless Day and Other Stories", "Pictorial Biography of William Shakespeare", "Wings of Dreams" and "A Late Sunrise, the Forgotten 18th August".

His poems and stories have been included in various anthologies like "Sea", "Moonlight", "If Love Happens Again", "Blooming Tales", "Victim of Past" and "Voices of Change".

Feroz Shaik

He has initiated a content series to groom young students reading habit. He's known for his simplistic writing style. He switches on the motivation besides teaching.

He is a Post Graduate in English language literature. He volunteered for (MAD....Make a difference) an NGO. He educates under privileged children during his free time.

He was born and raised in Vijayawada, the educational hub of Andhra Pradesh.

After his father's demise he did a lot of odd jobs, including shining mirrors, selling Papads, serving tea, etc. to feed his family.

His writings appeared in The Times of India (NIE) and The Hindu School Edition.

His interests include nature, birds, humor, photography and cycling.

Pratiksha Karn

Pratiksha Karn has been notably working on her writing career for 6 years. Her writing skills has a firm grip on criticism, observation on nature and mankind, satires, fate, love, patriotism. Her debut book "The locked episode" has sincere touch of her imaginative art and soul stirring words to express poetry. Besides, she is pursuing master degree in English from Vinobha Bhave University.

Ritika Mahto

Ritika Mahto is a young aspiring poet from Chakradharpur, Jharkhand. Born on 1st Feb,1998. She is an accountant by profession presently working in Bebbco Toyota, Jamshedpur.

She personally believes- "When you write, you not only frame words but you frame a story behind it".

She started writing at a very young age and she also have participated in many of the anthologies. Her beautiful poems and stories have been published with many renowned publishers.

She was inclined towards poetry and strives to capture attention of her readers through her words. She shares the different phases of life through her poems.

Instagram handle- @__ritzy__

Facebook handle - Ritika Vanshriyar

Samir Kumar Mandal

Textile Engineer by profession, Samir Kumar Mandal is working in a reputed organization for the last 25 years.

Coming from a rural background, he never forgets his roots. He was born and brought up with the ideas and ideals of Tagore and Vivekananda. He has strong work ethics and believes in simple living.

He likes to explore the intricacies and nuances of human relations. Though he is a forward-looking man, he likes to see any incident in hindsight. Readers may get some glimpses in his writing.

Samridhi Khanna

Samridhi Khanna is a 20-year-old passionate girl from Amritsar who is penning down her thoughts from late teenage. Her motivation for writing comes from her experiences and feelings. She started writing to express herself better. Her writings include one-liners, quotes, musing, short stories, and poetry. She posts the same from her Instagram page, i.e. @caprioco's phase. The word "caprioco" in literal terms has no meaning but she has attached a meaning to it. She explains it as a bubble where our minds are lost somewhere in some distinct dimension, which serves as a portal for insights, deep understandings, creativity, and ideas. She calls this intuitive bubble as her Caprioco's Phase. Samridhi knows more than 5 languages. She enjoys learning new languages which made her multilingual. She loves to fill colors in the blank canvases in her leisure time. She is an avid reader, nature enthusiast, a performer and a multitasker who strongly regards the fact "To live is to embrace the present moment and that's the key to ultimate joy and happiness."

Sathiyapriya Suriyanarayanan

Sathiyapriya Suriyanarayanan, an English Professor hails from Coimbatore region, Tamil Nadu. She is interested in writing poems and short stories in her native language Tamil and in English.

Her debut poem "Wall of Shame" got published in the anthology "Voices from the Society".

She is an award winning Tamil poet who is aspiring to pen down more in both the languages.

Sonali Mandal

Sonali Mandal (B.Sc., B.Ed.), has worked as a PRT in different schools for about 12 years and as a part-time abacus instructor for a year.

She stayed in many parts of the country, courtesy of her father and husband. This experience helped her to grow as an honest, open-minded and generous individual.

Now she is a homemaker. Writing short poems has always been one of her hobbies though this is her first publication.

Sri Harshika Gudlavilleti

Sri Harshika Gudlavilleti is a 'Book-Tuber' who reads, reviews and encourages people to read books through her very own YouTube channel- 'BOOK TALKIES'. She was born in Hyderabad and is at present living in Vijayawada, Andhra Pradesh. She is a class 8 student studying in 'Slate-The School', Vijayawada. She gets her daily dose of inspiration from people around her, especially her parents, sister, English teacher and a few of her friends at school. These are one of the initiators who rekindled her interests in weaving her thoughts into a perfect sentence!! The practice of writing Daily Dairy introduced by her school happens to be one of the prompters of bringing out the author in her childhood itself!! In her free time, she pens down her thoughts, reads books and experiments in kitchen. She cooks well and strongly believes in the quote – 'Failure is the stepping stone to Success', especially while experimenting in the kitchen!! She has her articles published in the student edition of the Times of India and is awaiting yet another publication in The Hindu, very soon. Thrillers like Sherlock Homes and Nancy Drew, books by Ruskin Bond and Sudha Murthy, 'Exam Warriors' authored by the Prime Minister, Sri. Modi Ji, (Through which she initiated her book reviews!!) are few of the top listings of this 13-year old optimistic teenager!!!

Sukriti Bansal

Sukriti Bansal is currently perusing mass communication from The Delhi School of Communication.

She is an artist, she likes to click and write about things she witnesses. She loves to read and write.

Vaishnavi Sistla

Vaishnavi Sistla is a 13-year-old, fun loving, daddy's girl of varied interests. She relishes savoring her grannys' hand-made food and enjoys family time. Her sister and parents are her pillars of support. She is happy when surrounded by her friends and likes chitchatting the most.

She is an avid reader. Amongst her favourite are – Enid Blyton (most favourite), Sudha Murthy, Thea Stilton, to name a few. No wonder her sister calls her a bookworm!

She is passionate about classical dance - Bharatanatyam, music - Carnatic and keyboard too, and is pursuing courses in the same. She is being guided by her teacher Mr. Feroz Shaik, who helps her in letting the juice of creativity flow through her pen.

Almost all good writing begins with terrible first efforts. You need to start somewhere - Anne Lamott. "Believe it or not" is Vaishnavi Sistla's first one. Hope you enjoyed reading it!!!